THE SEEING STICK

By Jane Yolen Pictures by Remy Charlip and Demetra Maraslis

THOMAS Y. CROWELL COMPANY   NEW YORK

For Ann Beneduce
with ten years of thanks and love—
Jane
And to the pleasure of new beginnings—
Demetra and Remy

OTHER BOOKS BY JANE YOLEN

The Bird of Time
The Girl Who Loved the Wind
The Wizard Islands
The Boy Who Had Wings
The Girl Who Cried Flowers and Other Tales
Rainbow Rider
The Magic Three of Solatia
The Transfigured Hart
The Moon Ribbon and Other Tales
Milkweed Days

COPYRIGHT© 1977 BY JANE YOLEN
ILLUSTRATIONS COPYRIGHT© 1977 BY
REMY CHARLIP AND DEMETRA MARASLIS
ALL RIGHTS RESERVED. EXCEPT FOR USE IN A REVIEW, THE REPRO-
DUCTION OR UTILIZATION OF THIS WORK IN ANY FORM OR BY ANY
ELECTRONIC, MECHANICAL, OR OTHER MEANS, NOW KNOWN OR
HEREAFTER INVENTED, INCLUDING XEROGRAPHY, PHOTOCOPYING,
AND RECORDING, AND IN ANY INFORMATION STORAGE AND
RETRIEVAL SYSTEM IS FORBIDDEN WITHOUT THE WRITTEN PER-
MISSION OF THE PUBLISHER. PUBLISHED SIMULTANEOUSLY IN
CANADA BY FITZHENRY & WHITESIDE LIMITED, TORONTO.
MANUFACTURED IN THE UNITED STATES OF AMERICA.
LIBRARY OF CONGRESS CATALOGING IN PUBLICATION DATA
YOLEN, JANE H   THE SEEING STICK.
SUMMARY: RELATES HOW AN OLD MAN TEACHES THE EMPEROR'S
BLIND DAUGHTER TO SEE.   [1. BLIND—FICTION.
2. CHINA—FICTION] I. CHARLIP, REMY, AND
DEMETRA MARASLIS.   II. TITLE.   PZ7.Y78Sc   [E]   75-6946
ISBN 0-690-00455-9   0-690-00596-2 (CQR)

Once in the ancient walled citadel of Peking
there lived an emperor who had only one daughter,
and her name was Hwei Ming.
Now this daughter had carved ivory combs
to smoothe back her long black hair.
Her tiny feet were encased in embroidered slippers,
and her robes were woven of the finest silks.
But rather than making her happy,
such possessions made her sad.
For Hwei Ming was blind,
and all the beautiful handcrafts in the kingdom
brought her no pleasure at all.
Her father was also sad
that his only daughter was blind,
but he could not cry for her.
He was the emperor after all,
and had given up weeping over such things
when he ascended the throne.
Yet still he had hope
that one day Hwei Ming might be able to see.
So he resolved that if someone could help her,
such a person would be rewarded
with a fortune in jewels.

He sent word of his offer
to the inner and outer cities of Peking
and to all the towns and villages
for hundreds of miles around.
Monks came, of course,
with their prayers and prayer wheels,
for they thought in this way
to help Hwei Ming see.
Magician-priests came, of course,
with their incantations and spells,
for they thought in this way
to help Hwei Ming see.
Physicians came, of course,
with their potions and pins,
for they thought in this way
to help Hwei Ming see.
But nothing could help.
Hwei Ming had been blind from the day of her birth,
and no one could effect a cure.

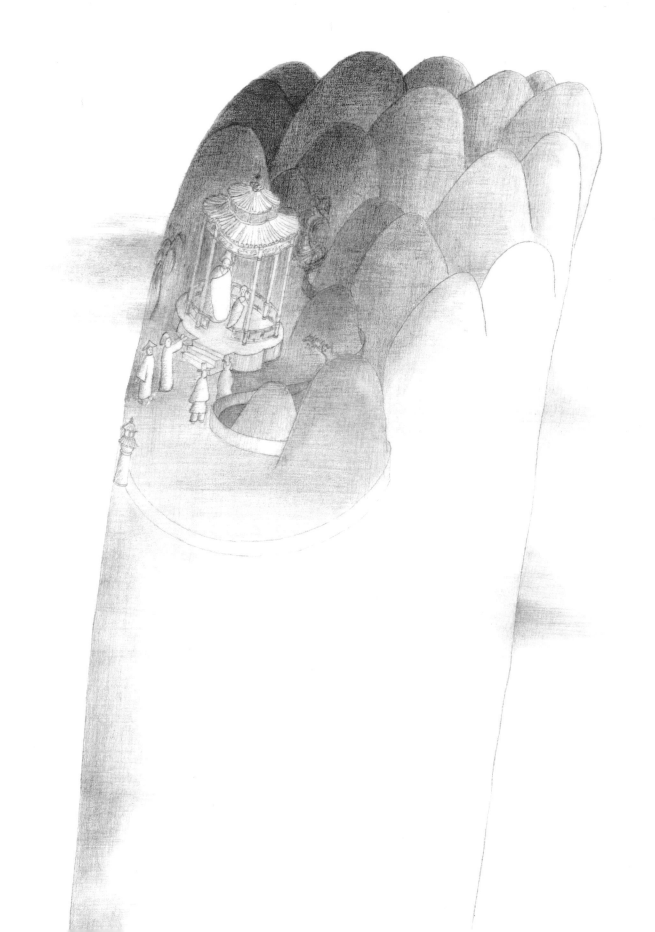

Now one day
an old man, who lived far away
in the south country,
heard tales of the blind princess.
He heard of the emperor's offer.
And so he took his few possessions —
a long walking stick,
made from a single piece of golden wood,
and his whittling knife —
and started up the road.
The sun rose hot on his right side
and the sun set cool on his left
as he made his way north to Peking
to help the princess see.

At last the old man,
his clothes tattered by his travels,
stopped by the gate of the Outer City.
The guards at the gate
did not want to let such a ragged old man in.
"Grandfather, go home.
There is nothing here for such as you," they said.
The old man touched their faces in turn
with his rough fingers.
"So young," he said,
"and already so old."
He turned as if to go.
Then he propped his walking stick
against his side
and reached into his shirt
for his whittling knife.
"What are you doing, grandfather?"
called out one of the guards
when he saw the old man bring out the knife.
"I am going to show you my stick, "
said the old man.
"For it is a stick that sees."
"Grandfather, that is nonsense,"
said the second guard.
"That stick can see no farther
than can the emperor's daughter."

"Just so, just so,"
said the old man.
"But stranger things have happened."
And so saying,
he picked up the stick
and stropped the knife blade back and forth
three times to sharpen its edge.
As the guards watched
from the gate in the wall,
the old man told them
how he had walked the many miles
through villages and towns
till he came with his seeing stick
to the walls of Peking.
And as he told them his tale,
he pointed to the pictures in the stick:
an old man,
his home,
the long walk,
the walls of Peking.
And as they watched further,
he began to cut their portraits into the wood.
The two guards looked at each other
in amazement and delight.
They were flattered at their likenesses
on the old man's stick.
Indeed, they had never witnessed such carving skill.

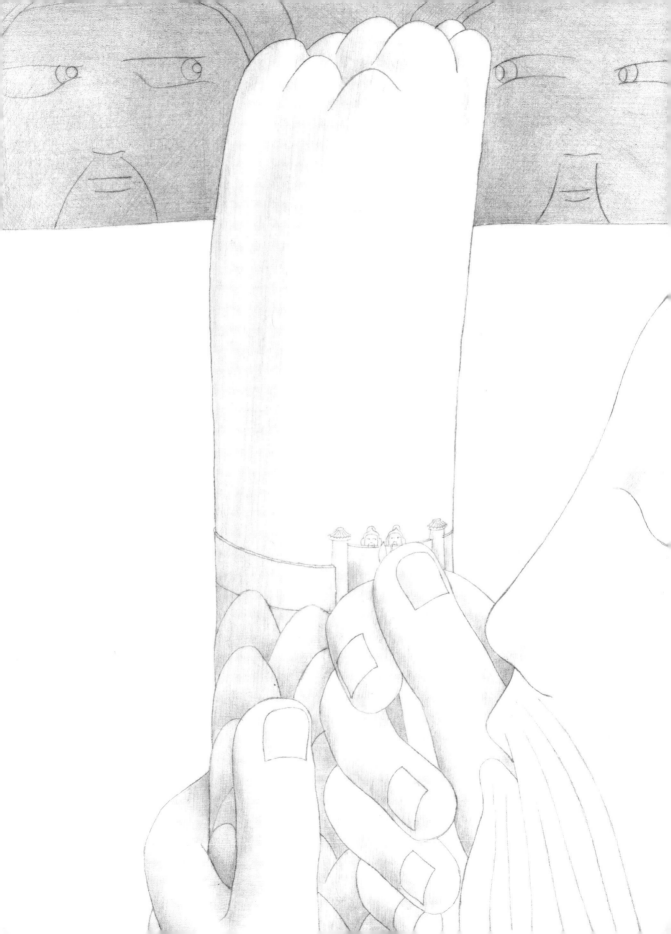

"Surely this is something
the guards at the wall
of the Inner City should see," they said.
So, taking the old man by the arm,
they guided him
through the streets of the Outer City,
past flower peddlers and rice sellers,
past silk weavers and jewel merchants,
up to the great stone walls.
When the guards of the Inner City
saw the seeing stick,
they were surprised and delighted.
"Carve our faces, too,"
they begged like children.
And laughing,
and touching their faces
as any fond grandfather would,
the old man did as they bid.
In no time at all,
the guards of the Inner City took the old man by his arm
and led him to the wall of the Innermost City
and in through the gate
to the great wooden doors of the Imperial Palace.

Now when the guards arrived
in the throne room of the Imperial Palace
leading the old man by the arm,
it happened that the emperor's blind daughter,
Hwei Ming,
was sitting by his side,
her hands clasped before her,
silent, sightless, and still.
As the guards finished telling
of the wonderful pictures carved on the golden stick,
the princess clapped her hands.
"Oh, I wish I could see that wondrous stick," she said.
"Just so, just so," said the old man.
"And I will show it to you.
For it is no ordinary piece of wood,
but a stick that sees."
"What nonsense," said her father
in a voice so low it was almost a growl.
But the princess did not hear him.
She had already bent toward
the sound of the old man's voice.
"A seeing stick?"

The old man did not say anything for a moment.
Then he leaned forward
and petted Hwei Ming's head
and caressed her cheek.
For though she was a princess,
she was still a child.
Then the old man began to tell again
the story of his long journey to Peking.
He introduced each character and object—
the old man,
the guards,
the great walls,
the Innermost City.
And then he carved the wooden doors,
the Imperial Palace,
the princess, into the golden wood.
When he finished,
the old man reached out
for the princess' small hands.
He took her tiny fingers in his
and placed them on the stick.
Finger on finger,
he helped her trace the likenesses.
"Feel the long flowing hair of the princess,"
the old man said.
"Grown as she herself has grown,
straight and true."
And Hwei Ming touched the carved stick.
"Now feel your own long hair," he said.
And she did.

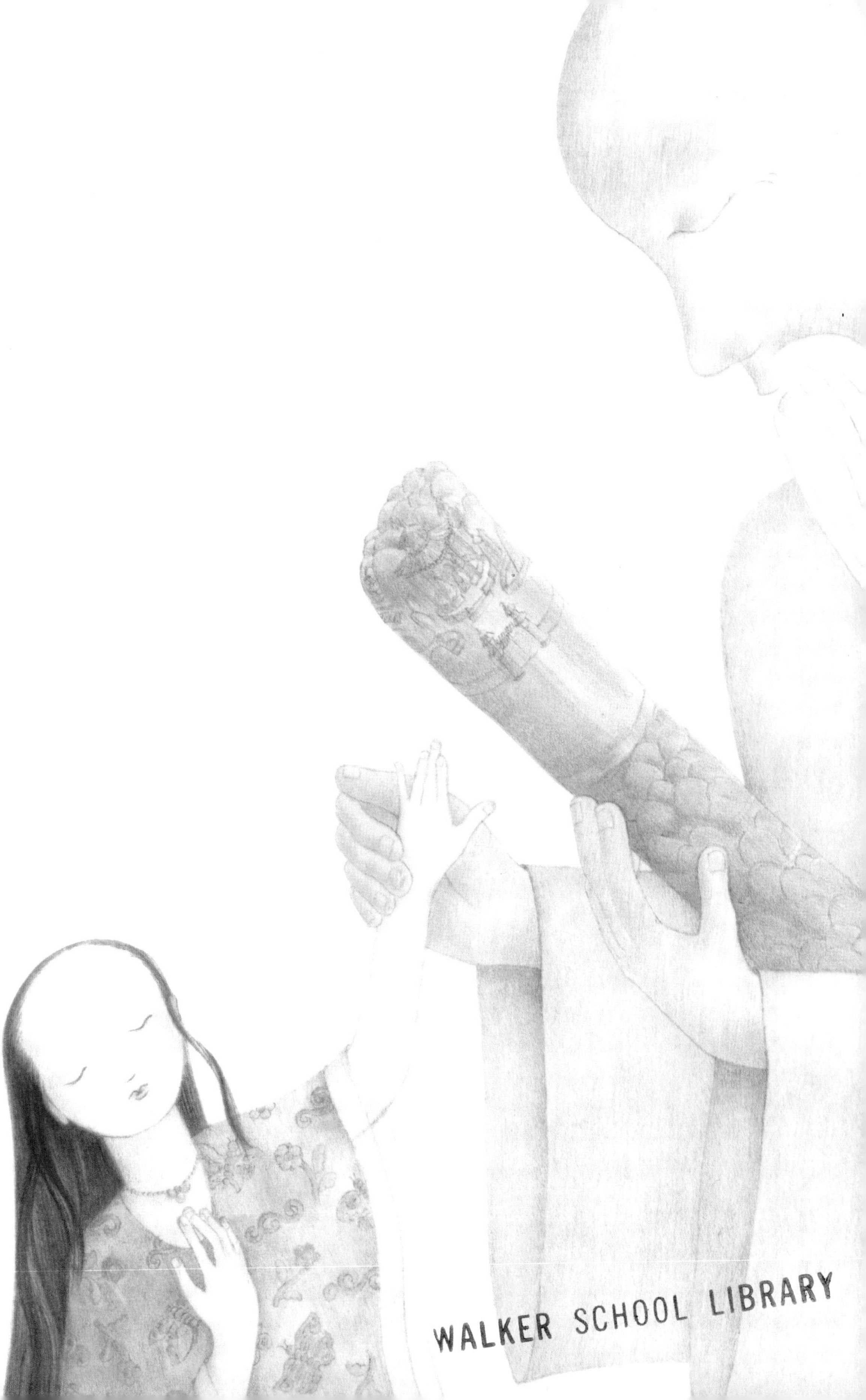

"Feel the lines in the old man's face," he said.
"From years of worry and years of joy."
He thrust the stick into her hands again.
And the princess' slim fingers
felt the carved stick.
Then he put her fingers onto his face
and traced the same lines there.
It was the first time
the princess had touched another person's face
since she was a very small girl.
The princess jumped up from her throne
and thrust her hands before her.
"Guards, O guards," she cried out.
"Come here to me."
And the guards lifted up their faces
to the Princess Hwei Ming's hands.
Her fingers,
like little breezes,
brushed their eyes and noses and mouths,
and then found each one on the carved stick.

Hwei Ming turned to her father,
the emperor,
who sat straight and tall
and unmoving on his great throne.
She reached out
and her fingers ran eagerly
through his hair
and down his nose and cheek
and rested curiously on a tear they found there.
And that was strange, indeed,
for had not the emperor
given up crying over such things
when he ascended the throne?

They brought her
through the streets of the city, then,
the emperor in the lead.
And Princess Hwei Ming
touched men and women
and children as they passed.
Till at last
she stood before the great walls of Peking
and felt the stones themselves.
Then she turned to the old man.
Her voice was bright
and full of laughter.
"Tell me another tale," she said.
"Tomorrow, if you wish," he replied.

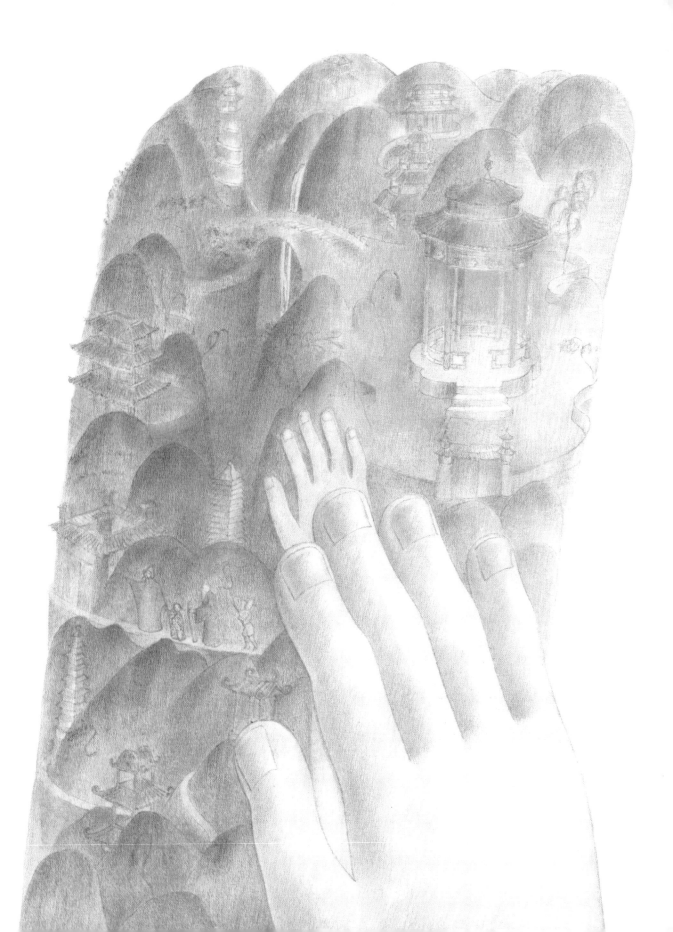

For each tomorrow
as long as he lived,
the old man dwelt
in the Innermost City,
where only the royal family stays.
The emperor rewarded him
with a fortune in jewels,
but the old man gave them all away.
Every day
he told the princess a story.
Some were tales as ancient
as the city itself.
Some were as new
as the events of the day.
And each time
he carved wonderful images
in the stick of golden wood.
As the princess listened,
she grew eyes
on the tips of her fingers.
At least that is what
she told the other blind children
whom she taught to see as she saw.
Certainly it was as true
as saying she had a seeing stick.
But the blind Princess Hwei Ming
believed that both things were true.
And so did all the blind children
in her city of Peking.

And so did the blind old man.

EGYPTIAN HIEROGLYPHS

FOR EVERYONE

An Introduction to the Writing of Ancient Egypt

by Joseph & Lenore Scott

BARNES
&NOBLE
BOOKS
NEW YORK

☥

Dedicated to Rose and Jessie, mothers of the authors.

ACKNOWLEDGMENT

The authors wish to express appreciation to Eric Young, who read the manuscript and gave constructive assistance in the final preparations for publication. Appreciation is also expressed for the kind permission of Oxford University Press to use selections from "*Egyptian Grammar*" by Sir Alan Gardiner, as well as various hieroglyphic signs, words and sentences from the same volume.

This edition published by Barnes & Noble, Inc.,
by arrangement with Harper Collins Publishers, Inc.

1993 Barnes & Noble Books

ISBN 1-56619-068-1

Printed and bound in the United States of America

M 9 8

*Sculptor's trial piece,
showing hieroglyphs used
in kings' titles*

CONTENTS

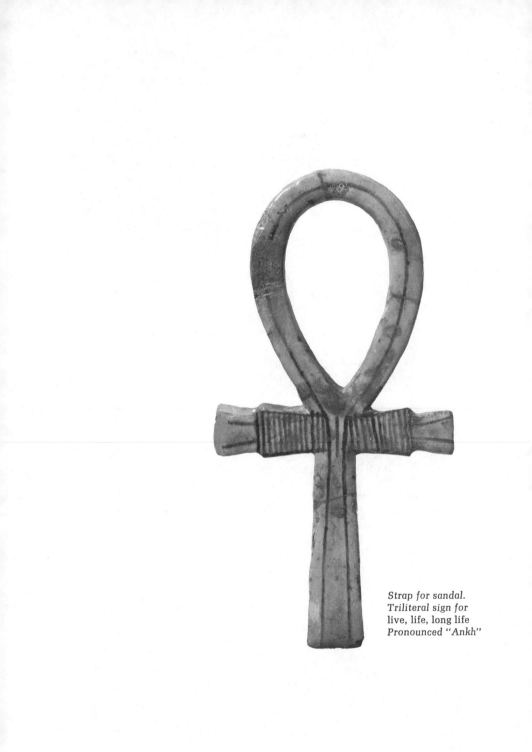

*Strap for sandal.
Triliteral sign for
live, life, long life
Pronounced "Ankh"*

FOREWORD

by the Chief Curator, Egyptian Museum

Cairo, U.A.R.

This book by Joseph and Lenore Scott is an excellent introduction to the fascinating realm of Egyptian hieroglyphs. It helps pull back the curtain which some people still believe shrouds the world of ancient Egypt. As Egyptologists know, and this book points out, hieroglyphs may be readily interpreted by persons who take the time and make the effort to study them. There is as much logic, grammatical structure, and literary excellence to be found in this ancient writing as in any modern language.

I believe this book will be valuable as an introduction to anyone seeking knowledge of Egyptian writing, whether in seeing museum collections, reading books, or visiting actual historic sites along the Nile. The book offers a simplified and interesting description of how hieroglyphs were written, gives a brief insight into their reading, and presents introductory information about many things that will be encountered in studying the language.

Because this book is well planned, attractively designed, and written especially for the layman beginning to learn about Egypt, I recommend it to any reader who wants an interesting and worthwhile investment of his time. By the end of the book, I believe the reader will be just as stimulated as the authors, Egyptologists, and myself in pursuing the subject as one of continuing interest. The study of hieroglyphs is a valuable and necessary tool in seeking to learn more about the remarkable peoples of ancient Egypt and their culture.

Mohammed H. Abd-ur-Rahman

*Typical Egyptian sculpture
has writing on its surface*

HOW TO START LEARNING

ABOUT HIEROGLYPHS

Whether your study of Egyptian hieroglyphs is brief or thorough, one thing is certain. It will introduce you to one of the most fascinating and unique periods in history—the world of ancient Egypt. By the time you finish this book, it is hoped you will want to explore that world even further.

It would require extensive study to gain a broad working knowledge of Egyptian hieroglyphic writing. Yet a broad knowledge of the writing is not necessary for you to enjoy the lore of Egypt. This book is intended to give you a basic knowledge of hieroglyphs and how to read them. If you decide to pursue your study of hieroglyphs beyond the pages of this book, you'll find that this field is broad indeed. There is not only an extensive vocabulary to be learned, but also a wealth of grammatical rules, several forms in which the language can be written, more than 3,000 picture-characters in hieroglyphic form, and many distinctive marks in the hieratic and demotic scripts (see page 74). Also, as in every language, there are special rules regarding usage. However, you need not concern yourself with all these things now. Your study of the basics of hieroglyphs contained in this book may be all you'll need to know for your own purposes.

How do the experts who have spent years in exhaustive study read hieroglyphs? This book will show you. Hieroglyphs are not only intelligible, but they present a workable form of writing. And although this form is not employed in the modern world, your study of it can be truly rewarding.

In starting to learn about Egyptian writing, some of the steps are:

> memorize the alphabet
> learn about biliterals
> study the determinatives
> recognize the direction of the writing
> learn how scholars pronounce words
> work with the vocabulary
> read the grammar section
> practice sentence writing

These are preliminary steps. The information given in the following pages is introductory and includes a large sampling of knowledge about the language and the writing. You can get a good idea about the ancient Egyptians' words just from what you read here.

To whom could you write in hieroglyphs today? Certainly not to the average Egyptian, because Arabic is the primary language spoken and written in Egypt today. Some Egyptians know English, French, or possibly another language, but very few know the ancient language represented by hieroglyphs. However, there are other people like yourself who are interested in hieroglyphs. Communication with fellow students of the language is not only fascinating, it will also give you an opportunity to put into practice what you have learned.

When did the Egyptians first begin to use hieroglyphs? No one knows for sure, but they have been identified on objects dating back to 3100 B.C. Hieroglyphic writing has been out of common use in Egypt for nearly 2,000 years. After the Arab conquest of Egypt in 640 A.D., Arabic became the dominant language of the Egyptians, replacing older languages and writing styles. It has remained dominant to the present day.

The terminology used to describe ancient Egyptian writing has become somewhat confused over the years. The words "hieroglyph" and "hieroglyphic" have not only come to be used interchangeably, but they are sometimes used incorrectly to describe the language of ancient Egypt. "Hieroglyph" is the noun form, and it is used to indicate only the writing style of ancient Egypt. "Hieroglyphic" is an adjective, and it should be

Many of these signs will soon be familiar

used only to describe that writing style. Thus you would say "I am studying hieroglyphs," or "I am studying hieroglyphic writing." But you would never say, "I am studying hieroglyphics." If you wanted to describe your study of the language, you would refer to it simply as the "ancient Egyptian language." There is no such thing as a "hieroglyphic language."

There have been several styles of writing the ancient Egyptian language. They are described later in the book. The formal style, and best known, is the hieroglyphic version. A script or handwritten version that was developed simultaneously is now called "hieratic." Several stages of change occurred in the handwritten form, so that over the passage of centuries the highly cursive form called "demotic" was evolved. Yet despite changes, all of the script styles have had a relationship to the hieroglyphs, just as modern handwritten scripts are related to the printed form of the regular alphabet.

And now turn to the alphabet, which is a good place to begin studying.

A well-made hieroglyph is a work of beauty

THE ALPHABET

One of the phenomena of Egyptian history is that the writing does not seem to have developed slowly, as is the case in other cultures. One moment it did not exist; then suddenly, indeed almost overnight the writing appeared fully developed. The earliest existing remains of the writing go back to the beginning of the First Dynasty, about 3100 B.C.

In early Egyptian writing, as typified by carvings on stone palettes, pictures as well as writing were used to tell a story. The illustrations were akin to acting out a message in a game of charades—each pose or picture conveyed an idea, event, or historic occasion. A man with an upraised club represented a warrior in battle. Several men running exemplified news that the enemy had been defeated and forced to flee. These illustrations are known as "ideograms" or "idea-o-grams."

It was not long before some of the ideograms were put to further use. As a theoretical example, if you wanted to talk about a bee, it might be logical to draw one 𐎜. Since you would also pronounce the verb "be" in the same way, the picture of the "bee" could represent "be," inasmuch as the words sound alike.

The same is true of the picture of a leaf 𓏲. If you were to combine this illustration with that of the bee, you could then pronounce the resulting picture-word of 𐎜 𓏲 as "bee-leaf," which spelled differently yet possessing the same sound would be "belief." With such a rebus principle, a new picture language would be formed. This is not an actual

Egyptian word, but shows how a writing style such as Egyptian hieroglyphs evolves.

In the example, the combined pictures formed words which were not related to the objects illustrated. A sound-picture such as this is known as a "phonogram," *phono* in Greek meaning sound or voice, and *gram* indicating "written." The "be," "bee," and "belief" explanations, as stated, are not actual words, yet show how picture writing is created.

The simplest Egyptian words were monosyllables, consisting of a consonant and a vowel. The sounds in these words came to be represented by pictorial signs. Soon the same signs were used to represent the sounds when they were used in more complex words. The association of the signs with the original objects was eventually lost in such usage.

For example, the most common monosyllabic word for owl was the consonant "m," plus a vowel. Since vowels were not written, the word could have been pronounced *em, am, im, om, um, me, ma, mi, mo,* or *mu.* In due course, every time an Egyptian wished to write the sign which represented the sound of "m," he drew a picture of an owl: ꞵ. This was the spelling of a sound, or a phonogram.

The same picture can be used in several ways. The hieroglyphic sign ⎯ looks as though it is the rippling surface of water. That is exactly what it represents in Egyptian writing. (However, the Hittites from the mountainous Near East regions used almost the same symbol to represent mountains.)

Also ⎯, the ripple, is a word in itself. Just as the Nile River flowed downstream toward other destinations and was the main transportation route, so the use of the water symbol ⎯ was convenient to show motion to or toward a person. The symbol therefore represented the preposition "to" or "toward," when applied to a human being (as distinct from toward a place). And finally, the ⎯ was employed to represent the alphabetic letter "n."

On the next page are the 24 letters of the ancient Egyptian alphabet. There are no written vowels in the language, although some letters seem to be similar to a few vowels used in the English language. They are usually considered consonants, although technically some letters are "semi-vowels." As mentioned before, true vowels were unwritten, but were inserted vocally by the Egyptians in the correct places while speaking. The same is true in today's Arabic, and other Semitic languages such as Hebrew.

THE HIEROGLYPH	WHAT IT REPRESENTS	SCHOLARS WRITE IT	HOW TO PRONOUNCE IT
vulture	ꜣ	a (father)
reed leaf	ỉ	i (filled)
or \\	two reed leaves	y	ee (discovery)
arm and hand	ꜥ	a (car) (broad a, as though gargling)
quail chick	w	oo (too), also w (wet)
foot	b	b (boot)
mat	p	p (pedestal)
horned viper	f	f (feel)
owl	m	m (moon)
water	n	n (noon)
mouth	r	r (right)
courtyard	h	h (hat)

14

THE HIEROGLYPH	WHAT IT REPRESENTS	SCHOLARS WRITE IT	HOW TO PRONOUNCE IT
	twisted flax	ḥ	h! (ha!)
	placenta (?)	ḫ	kh (Scotch "loch")
	animal's belly with teats	ẖ	ch (ch in German "ich")
or	folded cloth (a) or bolt of a door (b)	s	s (saw)
	pool	š	sh (show)
	hill slope	ḳ	k (key)
	basket with handle	k	k (basket)
	stand for a jar	g	g (go)
	loaf	t	t (tap)
	tethering rope	ṯ	tj (church)
	hand	d	d (dog)
	snake	ḏ	dj (adjust)

15

BILITERALS

Just as modern languages use symbols such as & % $ # @ ¢ as a convenient shorthand, the Egyptian language did the same. There were signs that represented combinations of two sounds. For instance, the "dj" sign was combined with the "ah" into a new symbol . It was still pronounced as were the original letters, "djah." Such a consolidation is called a biliteral, from *bi* (two) and *literal* (from the Latin *litera* or letter). The new sign for "djah" is that of a fire drill. When other words call for a "djah" sound the is still used, even though there is no longer a relationship of the newer word to the fire drill illustration.

Another example of biliteral is the m + n, or . This represents a word which was a gameboard used by the Egyptians for recreation. In due course, when an m + n were desired, the gameboard with moving pieces on top was shown: , even though the *mn* no longer referred to a game.

Sometimes three words or sounds were combined to form triliterals, such as *nefer*, which was written as . This, incidentally, is an actual word meaning beautiful, happy, or good. Read further, however, before using this triliteral just by itself. In this instance *nefer* is not only a triliteral, but a word as well.

The ancient hieroglyph writers took extra trouble to avoid confusion about their intentions. They used symbols that were sometimes repetitive and not pronounced. Even though is *nefer*, when written the *f* is repeated for emphasis, as well as the *r* , so that the word for happiness was actually shown as . However, the adding of the *f* and *r* illustrations could have additional uses. Sometimes a biliteral or triliteral might have two or even three sound values. Consequently, to indicate

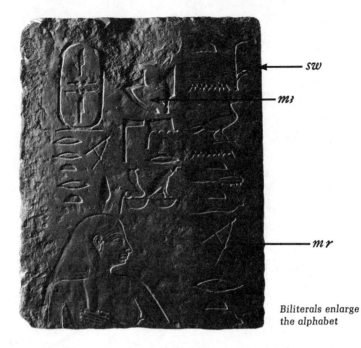

sw

mꜣ

mr

Biliterals enlarge the alphabet

which sound was to be read, one of the consonants was added, some-times two, and occasionally all of them. These are called "phonetic complements." Sometimes the added signs indicated changes of meaning or sound, but not always. The Egyptians loved symmetry, and wrote their hieroglyphs in squared patterns if aesthetics made it desirable, so it was common to add an extra sign to a biliterial or triliteral to complete such a pattern. This apparent redundancy occurs frequently in ancient Egyptian writing.

The exact style in which the alphabetic portions combine with the biliteral and triliteral signs varies. Sometimes the alphabetic characters precede the sign, and sometimes they follow it.

Here are the better-known biliterals. Most of the original objects depicted have been identified. A few are still unknown, or of uncertain portrayal, and are therefore marked "?." The transliteration given to the biliterals by Egyptologists is shown, and also the nearest English equiva-lent possible. The sounds in English are but a guide of convenience, especially formulated for this book. In case of uncertainty, the notation system used by Egyptologists should be the one that prevails. A descrip-tion of their sounds appears with the Alphabet on pages 14 and 15.

BILITERAL	COMBINES THESE	ILLUSTRATION	PRONOUNCED	
		Backbone, with spinal cord	*ꜣw*	aoo
		Chisel or hairpin	*ꜣb*	ab
		Newborn hartebeest (antelope)	*iw*	yoo
		(Unknown)	*im*	im
		Fish	*in*	in
		Eye	*ir*	ir
		Bundle of reeds	*is*	is
		Horizontal wooden column	*ꜥꜣ*	aa
		Cormorant	*ꜥk*	ak
		Spool filled with twine	*ꜥḏ*	adj
		Lasso	*wꜣ*	wa
		One-barbed harpoon	*wꜥ*	wah
		Horns of ox	*wp*	wep
		Desert hare	*wn*	wen
		Flower (?)	*wn*	wen
		Swallow or martin	*wr*	wer
		Cord wound on stick	*wḏ*	wedj
		Jabiru, or wood ibis	*bꜣ*	ba
		Elephant tusk	*bḥ*	beh!
		Pintail duck, flying	*pꜣ*	pa
		House	*pr*	per
		Hind-quarters of lion or leopard	*pḥ*	peh!

Biliteral mn: is silhouette of game board similar to this one

BILITERAL	COMBINES THESE	ILLUSTRATION	PRONOUNCED	
		Sickle	*mꜣ*	maa
		Milk jug, carried in net	*mi*	mee
		Forearm with hand, holding loaf	*mi*	mee
		Three water ripples	*mw*	moo
		Game board silhouette	*mn*	men
		Hoe	*mr*	mer
		Chisel or hairpin. Same as *ꜣb*	*mr*	mer
		Whip	*mḥ*	meh!
		Three fox skins tied together	*ms*	mes
		Vulture	*mt*	met
		Phallus	*mt*	met
		Adze and bowl	*nw*	noo

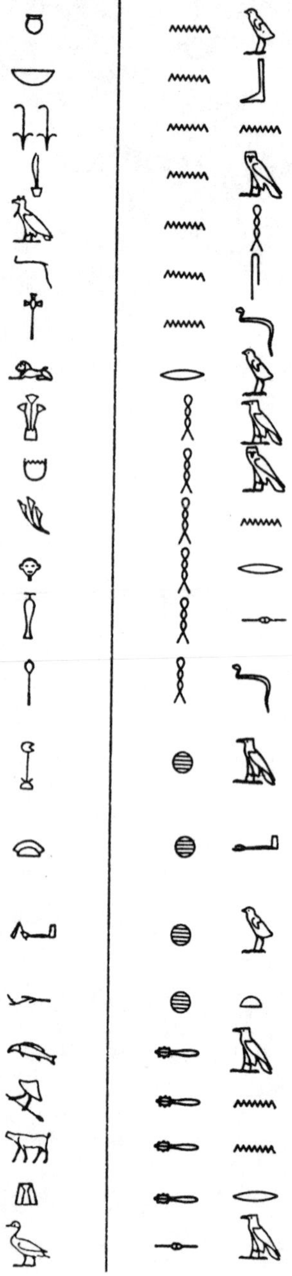

BILITERAL / COMBINES THESE	ILLUSTRATION	PRONOUNCED	
	Bowl	*nw*	noo
	Wicker basket	*nb*	neb
	Rush with shoots	*nn*	nen
	Butcher's knife	*nm*	nem
	Guinea-fowl	*nḥ*	neh!
	Tongue of an ox (?)	*ns*	nes
	(Unknown)	*nḏ*	nedj
	Resting lion	*rw*	roo
	Clump of papyrus	*ḥꜣ*	ha
	Well filled with water	*ḥm*	hem
	Herb	*ḥn*	hen
	Face	*ḥr*	her
	Tall water pot	*ḥs*	hes
	Tall staff with pear-shaped head	*ḥḏ*	hedj
	Roots, stalk, leaf of lotus plant	*ḫꜣ*	kha
	Hill, with rising sun behind	*ḫꜥ*	kha
	Forearm, with hand holding whip	*ḫw*	khoo
	Branch	*ḫt*	khet
	Oxyrhynchus fish	*ẖꜣ*	kha
	Arms engaged in rowing	*ẖn*	khen
	Skin of a goat	*ẖn*	khen
	Butcher's block	*ẖr*	kher
	Pintail duck	*sꜣ*	sa

BILITERAL	COMBINES THESE	ILLUSTRATION	PRONOUNCED	
		(Unknown)	*s*ɂ	sa
		Upper-Egypt plant	*sw*	soo
		Two-barbed arrow head	*sn*	sen
		Swab made from hank of fibre	*sk*	sek
		Cow's skin pierced by arrow	*st*	set
		Pool with lotus flowers	*š*ɂ	sha
		Feather	*šw*	shoo
		Loop of cord, ends downward	*šn*	shen
		Loop of cords, ends up	*šs*	shes
		Water skin	*šd*	shed
		Arms, extended	*k*ɂ	ka
		Censer for fumigation	*kp*	kep
		Piece of crocodile skin	*km*	kem
		Bricklayers' instrument (?)	*ḳd*	qed
		Black ibis	*gm*	gem
		(Unknown)	*gs*	ges
		Potter's kiln	*t*ɂ	ta
		Pestle	*tì*	tee
		Sledge	*tm*	tem
		Duckling	*t̠*ɂ	tja
		Fire drill	*ḏ*ɂ	dja
		Mountain (or valley?)	*ḏw*	djoo
		Bundle of flax, with bolls	*ḏr*	djer
		Imitates tied bundle of stalks	*ḏd*	djed

*Determinatives help make
continuous writing readable*

DETERMINATIVES

The Egyptian scribes had the problem of making sure that their written words conveyed the exact meaning intended. To produce the clarity they wanted, the writers added picture-signs at the end of many words. These were not generally pronounced. They were primarily to help the reader *determine* the exact meaning of the word. Appropriately, the added illustrations have become known as "determinatives." See the following pages for some popular ones.

Since vowels were not written, and individual consonant signs could have several meanings until clarified, determinatives assisted in this function. It is as though the English letters s + n were shown as sn, with the vowel missing. These letters could represent son, sun, and soon. But if a picture of a man or a sundisk was drawn after each one, the meanings could be differentiated.

Also determinatives could be used as abbreviations for an entire word. Thus 𓃀 meant "horse," even though this particular word might be written at least two different ways, when spelled in full. The same for ship 𓊝. This symbol was also used as the determinative with several words for boat, or was occasionally used just by itself.

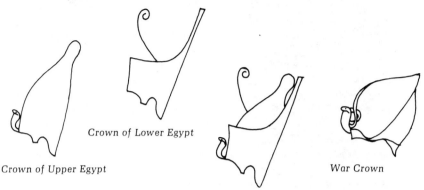

Crown of Lower Egypt

Crown of Upper Egypt

War Crown

Double Crown of Unified Egypt

Determinatives are used with almost every word. A word indicating that someone is walking, running, or advancing toward an object, is often followed by the determinative ⅄ , which of course represents legs.

Since happiness is a human emotion, the determinative of a human being showing emotion is often that of a person's face added to the regular word for "rejoice":

When an intangible thought is to be illustrated, a sign is needed to show that the word is a product of the mind. A determinative is employed which represents this fact, such as a papyrus scroll, shown neatly rolled up and tied with a ribbon ❙ . If an Egyptian wrote a word associated with hearing, the ear of an ox was often used:

Determinatives serve another useful purpose. There were no separations between words in an Egyptian sentence. The pictures followed each other in continuous sequence, without a break for spacing. Since the determinatives came only at the ends of words, they also serve to divide the writing into recognizable words and sentences, even though the signs seem to be linked endlessly. Sometimes, however, a rubric was used as a sentence ending or beginning. A rubric was written in red, whereas the rest of the text was in black.

Each of the illustrations used in the determinatives showed something familiar in the lives of the ancient Egyptians. The same is true of all other hieroglyphs. Notice the men, for instance. Not only are there men standing and sitting, but they are also shown in many types of activities. Parts of the body are also utilized, such as the face, eyes, ears, mouth, arms, legs, hands, fingers, and feet. Women are also used in numerous determinatives.

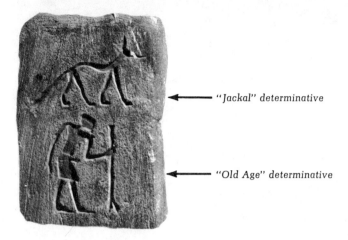

"Jackal" determinative

"Old Age" determinative

Animals are employed profusely. Sometimes the pictures created genuine conflicts. When an animal was drawn on a tomb wall, its soul could enter the picture in the next life, enabling the animal in the illustration to come to life. But what would happen, wondered the ancient Egyptians, if the animal should wander away when the owner of the tomb wanted it? This was easily solved. In many tombs the hieroglyphs representing animals were carved or drawn to show them without legs or without heads. In this way the animals could not run away, nor could they eat the food placed in the tomb, which was intended for the owner's sole use. Evil animals such as snakes were dismembered to render them harmless. At other times, the injury or decapitation was to convey an idea or represent a sound, uses beyond regular illustration needs.

Also notice the representation of other familiar objects, such as trees, plants, buildings, ships, furniture, clothing, and instruments of warfare. In addition, the Egyptians used illustrations of agricultural implements, baskets, kitchenware, and various types of foods.

There were symbols depicting the sky, sun, stars, and moon. Some other representations included temple furniture, sacred emblems, crowns, beads, sandals, rope, jars, and buildings.

To show two or more objects, such as men, the determinative was originally repeated as many times as needed. If there were 12 men, then a dozen men were drawn. Before long, the accepted way to show a plurality of objects came via the adding of three vertical lines ⲓ ⲓ ⲓ. This indicated a multiplicity of items shown, without stating an exact number, such as numerous men 🕴 or many houses ⬠.

Here are a few of the many determinatives used by Egyptian scribes, stone carvers, and artists:

HIEROGLYPH	ILLUSTRATES	USED AS DETERMINATIVE TO INDICATE:
	Seated man	Man; man's relationships or occupations
	Man with hand to mouth	Eating and drinking. Functions involving mouth or head
	Man hiding behind wall	Hiding
	Tired man sinking to ground	Weariness, tiredness, faintness
	Man carrying basket on head	To carry, work, load up
	Man with arms tied behind back	Enemy, rebel, foreigner
	Man falling	Fallen enemy, to fall
	Child sucking thumb	Child, orphan, to be young
	Old man with cane	Old man, old, to lean, elder
	Man with pole in hand	Man in authority, official
	Man striking with stick	Strong, plunder, teach, strike
	Man with upraised arms	High, be high, rejoice, extol
	Man dancing	Dance, joy, jubilate
	Man with bundle on stick	Wanderer, herdsman, stranger
	Seated god	God (Note beard, straight wig)
	King	King (Note straight beard, hair, and asp on forehead)

	Recumbent mummy	Death, sarcophagus
	Seated woman	Woman, female, wife
	Pregnant woman	Pregnant, to conceive
	Head profile	Head, nod
	Eye	Eye, to see
	Eye with flowing tears	To cry, weep
	Part of human face	Nose, to smell, face, take pleasure, enjoy
	Liquid coming from lips	Spit, spew out, vomit
	Arms extended downward	Embrace, envelop
	Arms extended, as in negation	Be ignorant of, do not know
	Arm holding loaf, or bowl	Give, present, offer
	Hand in fist	Grasp, seize
	Legs walking	Walk, step, run
	Legs walking backwards	Move backwards, turn back, retreat
	Bull	Bull, ox, cattle
	Horse	Horse
	Ram	Ram, sheep
	Cat	Cat
	Greyhound	Dog, hound
	Jackal	Jackal, dignitary, worthy

Determinatives are everywhere in Egyptian texts. This tablet contains many

HIEROGLYPH	ILLUSTRATES	USED AS DETERMINATIVE TO INDICATE:
	Giraffe	Giraffe, to foretell
	Head of angry bull	Rage
	Head, neck of long-necked animal	Throat, swallow, be parched
	Elephant tusk	Tooth, to bite, laugh
	Ox ear	To hear
	Cow's skin	Hide, leather, skin, rug
	Intestine	To turn, to go round
	Vulture	Vulture, terror
	Lapwing bird, with twisted wings	'Common folk'

HIEROGLYPH	ILLUSTRATES	USED AS DETERMINATIVE TO INDICATE:
	Sparrow	Small, narrow, bad, defective, empty
	Goose	Bird, be idle, delay, talk, perish
	Lizard	Lizard, "many of," and related words
	Crocodile	Crocodile, greedy, lust after
	Fish	Fish, smell, stink
	Fly	Fly
	Tree	Tree, tent
	Branch	Wood, trees, wooden objects
	Palm branch, stripped of leaves	Be young, vigorous
	Reeds, side by side	Marshland, country, peasant
	Heap of corn	Heaps, overflow
	Vine on props	Vine, wine, gardener, fruit
	Thorn	Thorn, sharp, and related words
	Top of gateway	Sky
	Sky with suspended sceptre	Night, darkness, dusk
	Moisture falling from sky	Rain, dew, rainstorm
	Sun	Sun, day, time period
	Sun with rays	Sunshine
	Star	Star, to teach
	Tongue of land	Sand bank, land, shore
	Hill country	Foreign land, hill country, desert

The sacred ibis is a determinative in the name for the ibis-headed god Thoth

HIEROGLYPH	ILLUSTRATES	USED AS DETERMINATIVE TO INDICATE:
	Road bordered by shrubs	Road, and related words, travel
	Three ripples	Water, liquid, wave, drink, brook
	Well full of water	Well, pool
	House	House, building, room, interior, sanctuary, tomb
	Hall of columns	Hall of columns, office
	Gateway	Door, gateway
	Door bolt, walking legs	Words implying motion: go, send, bring
	Falling wall	Overthrow, demolish, tilt
	Stairway	Stairway, terraced hill
	Village with crossroads	Village, town
	Boat on water	Boat, ship, travel by water, sail downstream
	Boat upside down	Overturn, upset
	Ship sailing	Sail upstream
	Sail	Breath, wind, sail

HIEROGLYPH	ILLUSTRATES	USED AS DETERMINATIVE TO INDICATE:
	Seat	Seat, place
	Coffin	Coffin, bury
	Brazier with rising flame	Flame, heat, cook, torch
	White crown of Upper Egypt	White crown, Upper Egypt
	Red crown of Lower Egypt	Red crown, Lower Egypt
	Combined crowns	Double crown, Upper and Lower Egypt
	Collar of beads	Gold, silver, precious metal
	Cloth with fringe	Clothe, cloth, clothing, conceal
	Axe	Axe, to cut, hew
	Throwing stick, club	To throw, to create or form, foreign country or person
	Fishing net	To net animals, hold; field laborer
	Knife	Knife, be sharp, cut down, carve
	Hoe	Cultivate, hack up, love
	Coil of rope	Rope, drag, tie, actions with rope
	Cup	Cup, unite, in company of
	Water pouring from water pot	Be cool, to cool off
	Beer jug	Beer, be drunk, pot, tribute
	Papyrus scroll, tied and sealed	Writing, and things written, truth, to know, great
	Paint palette, paint pot, brush holder	Scribe, to write

THE NARMER PALETTE

Both sides of the cosmetic palette of King Narmer, I Dynasty, about 3100 B.C., are shown. Although this is one of the oldest surviving historical records of early Egypt, it presents a number of fully developed hieroglyphs, in addition to pictures which tell their own story. The slate portrays the victory of the southern king over inhabitants of the northern papyrus-growing delta land.

Bottom four rows are read toward
the faces of the animals, right to
left. Upper panels show three
writing directions: right to left,
left to right, and down

WRITING DIRECTION

In which direction should hieroglyphs be read? In any of four ways.
The Egyptians usually wrote from right to left. But in other instances,
the ancient scribe or stone chiseler went from left to right. On still other
occasions and especially on doorways and stone shafts, the writing was
downward. In some cases of vertical printing, two characters are placed
side by side. Thus the reader has to know whether to read the left or the
right of the two characters first. There is an easy way to determine the
direction. *Read from the direction toward which the people or animals
are facing.* If the faces look toward the left, start reading from the left.

In the illustrations, all styles of writing are shown. By reading the
pictures in numerical order, you can see the correct sequence. Notice
that no matter which way you read, the final sequence of characters is
the same. When one sign is above another, the top one is read first.

In addition, observe the artistry with which the scribe tried to group
the hieroglyphs. Wherever you see ancient Egyptian writing, you will
not encounter unsightly space gaps. For instance, where the word for
sky requires a ▫ plus ◠ plus the determinative for heaven ▭, instead
of stringing them in a line, ▫ ◠ ▭ , writers grouped them. The scribes

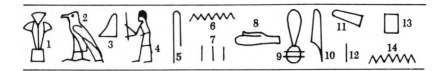

Left to right, as one line

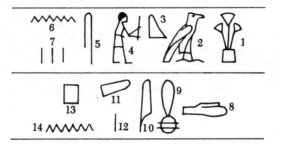

Right to left, in two lines

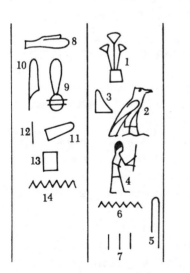

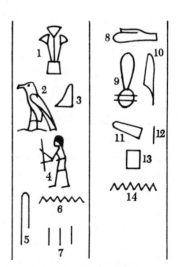

Read down, right to left   Read down, left to right

Read from right to left

knew that the low characters would look better, when next to tall figures, if some low symbols were placed on top of each other. It gave the effect of height, saved space, and improved the appearance. Artistic liberties were therefore permitted, and even desirable. Therefore sky was written

On door frames, the Egyptians often expressed their love of symmetry by writing inscriptions on each side of the entrance using the same text. To keep the balance, the hieroglyphs on the right side faced toward the door, and those on the left side faced that way too. The effect was to make one text seem the mirror image of the other.

Actually there were still other directions for writing. Some extreme instances show inscriptions that read backwards, the retrograde motion being the opposite of the expected reading direction. On the bottom of bowls, or on circular mirrors, inscriptions are written along the circle's edge.

When text accompanies the figure of a human being, the writing usually faces in the same direction as that in which the head is turned.

In modern typesetting, hieroglyphic writing is read from left to right. This is to simplify reading when accompanying a western language.

Pharaoh Sesostris III of XII Dynasty.

The two vertical columns are read
top to bottom, away from the legs.

Both say: "The Horus, Ntr-hprw,
King of Upper and Lower Egypt,
Kha-kau-re, beloved of Horus
of Nekhen, Given Life."

Ability to read and write was highly admired, often leading to advancement not otherwise possible

THE SCRIBE

Few Egyptians could read or write. Many were living in virtual serfdom. There was little interest for the average person in the world beyond the limits of the neighboring village. The lower classes had almost no incentive to learn to read or write, nor generally even the opportunity.

Many Egyptian boys, however, had the ambition to become a scribe. So rare was it to find a literate person, in fact, that someone familiar with the written language soon gained local prominence. Becoming a scribe was a major route for escaping the drudgery of manual labor. Being a scribe also offered the possibility of becoming a minor government official, a representative of a nobleman, or doing one of the many jobs that required the skills of a writer or bookkeeper. Within the religious hierarchy there were many positions open for scribes. Therefore the ability of the parents to afford education for their son, and the sponsorship he received from persons able to help him, were important for becoming a scribe. Girls had little chance of obtaining an education or advancement as might befall a scribe, yet it was not impossible.

Many scribes became bookkeepers or clerks. Most of the land was owned by nobles, the royal family, or religious shrines. These offered the main opportunities, and with such an association an educated scribe could quickly come to be looked upon as a person of importance. The scribes kept the records of the flocks, crops, workers, and materials used. They were important figures during pyramid building, in construction of buildings, and in keeping merchants' records of cloth, sandals, furniture production, and grain storage. For others there were records of export and import trade with other Mediterranean or Mesopotamian countries.

The scribes were the secretaries and civil servants of 5,000 to 2,000 years ago.

Opportunities for their advancement were occasionally good, although limited by the dominance of the nobility, royalty, and priesthood which occupied the more significant positions in Egypt. However, when a nobleman needed a new manager or a representative, what was more natural than to call upon the educated man who was familiar with his immediate problems—the scribe? The training for scribehood could be well worth the trouble.

Learning to write and read Egyptian hieroglyphs required more than a casual effort. Long years of study were needed. When a boy was accepted for training, he was placed in scribal school. There were many routine jobs to keep him quite busy, even if he did not advance far. If he were good at his studies, he might look forward to being taken into the apprenticeship of an older scribe, which could further his advancement.

The alphabet of the hieroglyphs was not like the simple 26-letter alphabet of the English language. There were literally hundreds of picture signs. These represented sounds, combinations of sounds, and ideas as expressed in determinatives.

The minimum language requirement, to begin to read or write, included at least 200 hieroglyphs. One list of signs used by an apprentice scribe has been found containing more than 450 characters. A fairly broad knowledge of the language called for about 750 picture signs. A reasonably extensive knowledge of hieroglyphs would have included 3,000 or more signs, although many would be rarely used.

Did the scribe have a quicker way to write, other than to draw the hieroglyphs? Yes. If you had attended scribe school as a young Egyptian, you would have been taught the "freehand" hieratic, which was the script form of hieroglyphs. Your writing implements would have been wooden tablets, chips of limestone, or pottery. You would not have used expensive papyrus until you were well advanced.

WRITING TOOLS

The sign associated with writing shown here illustrates the three tools of the ancient Egyptian writer. First is a pen case, tall and slender to hold the long brushes of the writer. Next is a jar of water for softening the paint. Finally there is the palette with two cakes of paint or ink, one black and the other usually red. A string connects all three so that the scribe could carry them in hand, or sling them over his shoulder.

Most palettes were made of wood, and the finer ones of ivory. A slender rush, which served as the pen, was either softened at one end to act as a brush, or else cut to form a hard point. If cut, one edge was broad for drawing heavy lines, and the other edge fine for thin lines.

When an Egyptian wrote, he used many types of materials. There are, of course, many fine examples of hieroglyphs carved into stone and wood, and impressed into metal. The "freehand" hieratic or demotic writing is typically found on pottery, linen, and papyrus.

Papyrus was customarily made in flat sheets, about a foot long. Two layers of strips cut from the stem of the papyrus reeds from the marshlands were pressed together, at right angles. In making a scroll, 20 of them were usually joined together. (One existing scroll is 130 feet long.) The writing was done in lines which were kept to a reasonable width so that the eye scan would not be too long. Occasionally the second side of a scroll would be used if more space was needed. If a scroll was used on both sides, the side which had the reeds running horizontally usually received the more important writing. This side was also preferred because scribes found it easier to write on the papyrus fibers when they were horizontal to the writer.

Although papyrus is the source of our word for *paper*, modern paper is made of wood and cotton fibers, a development of the Chinese rather than the Egyptians.

Papyrus was hard to make, and therefore not wasted. For ordinary letters and business transactions, small pieces of stone or broken pottery often proved cheaper and just as satisfactory. In later Coptic times, for school work, a board was covered with wax upon which a bone or wood stylus could impress the writing. To erase, the wax was merely pressed smooth again.

The red paint served a useful purpose for the scribe. Primarily it was used for rubrics at the end of a sentence, although such endings could usually be adequately shown in the ordinary black as well. Occasionally the names of deities were written in this contrasting color also. In addition, hieroglyphs made for public viewing were often written in several colors, even though black was by far the more predominant writing ink.

Several techniques for inscribing hieroglyphs can be seen when viewing monuments, public buildings, tombs, and mummy cases:

1. A drawing might be made in outline with the writing tool, then painted. This was a flat-surface illustration.

2. Hieroglyphs could be sculptured into a hard surface, and then painted when finished.

3. Occasionally the signs could be carved into the surface, but not colored. However, where such plain hieroglyphs are found it is usually because the ravages of time and weather have obliterated the original coloring.

Some of the coloring consists of one tint throughout, such as red. Or, more commonly, blue was used on earlier monuments. On many words, the practice developed of using numerous colors. The artists endeavored to imitate the traditional color of each object. The moon was yellow, the hills red, the sky blue. Men were given red flesh and white clothing, with the fabric folds sometimes in red. Women were in yellow, wearing red or green dresses. Animals were painted in their normal colors, such as a lion in yellow, and a jackal in black.

With such coloration, many tombs and mummy cases presented a gay, artistic effect. So much effort was required for the elaborate work that it was usually confined to works of great importance, or to instances where the payments that could be made by the commissioner of the work were the deciding factor. For the ordinary coffin, tablet, or papyrus, black was the predominant ink for writing, with red for the rubrics at sentence endings.

PRONUNCIATION

The ancient Egyptian language shows affinities to Semitic tongues, such as Arabic and Hebrew, yet it is not Semitic. It is also related to the Hamitic languages of North Africa, yet it is not Hamitic. For convenience it is described as belonging to the Hamito-Semitic linguistic group.

In Egyptian, the vowels are not expressed in written form. Since the consonants by themselves are not generally pronounceable without vowels, and the proper original vowels are not known, readers of the ancient writing have had a difficult problem. It has been solved insofar as practical needs are concerned by inserting an "e" wherever there seems a need for a vowel. This is recognized as being an expedient, however, rather than accurately representing the original sounds.

As an example, take the word for joy: ⬭𝄢 ⌒ 𝄞𝄽 . It consists of an r⬭, sh⬭, w𝄞, and t ⌒ , plus two determinatives 𝄞𝄽 , which are not

*First it is necessary to know whether a sign is alphabetic,
determinative, phonetic or ideographic*

pronounced. If you were speaking to a modern Egyptologist and pronounced the word as *reshwet,* you would be correct.

For accuracy in speaking the original tongue, relate the common English vowels of a, e, i, o, u to the Egyptian consonants. How would you pronounce these letters: *gd* ? Your choice of available vowels could fit in between the two letters, as well as before or after them. Should the word be *egad, eged, oged, god, ged, gud, gid gido, gedaa, egoda,* or some other combination? Most of the time, it is just not known. All that is available for reading is the written symbol . Therefore the modern Egyptologists make it pronounceable by adding an "e," resulting in the word being spoken as "ged."

There are occasions when scholars know exactly where to insert other vowels, or how the original sounded, by having found certain words carried into other languages such as Greek, Hebrew, Akkadian, and Latin. Such words are generally proper names, such as royal, divine, private, or geographic titles.

The sounds of many common words are traceable through Coptic. The Copts were Christian descendants of the ancient Egyptians. *Copt* is a corruption of the Greek word for Egypt, *Aiguptos*. The Macedonians, under Alexander the Great, captured Egypt in 332 B.C., were followed by the Romans in 30 B.C., and later by the Arabs in 640 A.D. After the arrival of the Arabs, Coptic was gradually replaced by Arabic, and as a spoken language had generally disappeared by the 16th century. However, as late as 1870 Coptic was still spoken in a few small, out-of-the-way Christian villages in Upper Egypt, and is still spoken in Coptic churches today, even if not commonly understood.

Comparing Coptic to the original Egyptian language is akin to comparing modern English to sounds of Anglo-Saxon words a thousand years ago, or even Chaucerian English of 600 years ago. Spoken languages are constantly in a state of flux and change. Pronunciation, dialects, accents, grammar, and usage are continually being altered as well as affected by contemporary languages. By the beginning of the Christian Era, Coptic employed a large amount of Greek. Nevertheless, it continued to bear a relationship to ancient Egyptian. By that time the familiar hieroglyphic writings of the famed XVIII and XIX Dynasties of the New Kingdom were at least 1,200 years old, which was twice as old as Chaucer's writings are today.

From a philological standpoint, Coptic is important in that it was the only form of Egyptian in which vowels were regularly written. Yet the language is a very late stage of the country's tongue. The vocabulary includes many Greek words, and the word order is more Greek than Egyptian. Coptic became a semi-artificial literary language elaborated by the native Christian monks. The first efforts to associate the language with Greek letters occurred in the second century, A.D., during which time subjects such as horoscopes, magical texts, and the like were put into writing. Compounding the use of Coptic for pronunciation is the fact that several regional dialects were employed.

Next to Coptic, the most important sources for determining how Egyptian was pronounced are the contemporary languages of nearby countries. In all of them, vowels were written. Consequently, when Egyptian names and words were mentioned in those nations, they were reproduced in the other languages by the writer as he thought he heard

*Shawabties as these
accompanied the casket, ready to
reply to the god Osiris in
behalf of the deceased*

them. The appropriate word endings for that language were often affixed to the original Egyptian word, so that the reproduction did not always resemble the original sound. This was true in the Greek regions, as well as those where Hebrew, Akkadian, and Hittite were spoken.

For example, when a Hebrew writer heard the Egyptian refer to the king as *per-aa* 𓉐, his own rendition in Hebrew was constructed so as to pronounce the word *Pharaoh*. When the Greek historian Herodotus heard the Egyptian names for the famed IV Dynasty Pharaoh Khufu, who built the largest of the pyramids, and for the gods Ese and Wosi(r), he reproduced them with Greek endings to make them *Cheops, Isis,* and *Osiris*. Therefore when you occasionally encounter an apparent conflict in words, you might be witnessing the Egyptian word alongside a foreigner's interpretation and variation of that word.

"Papyrus scroll"
šfdw, pronounced "sefdoo"

VOCABULARY

The words shown in the following list are representative of the ancient Egyptian language. There is no complete dictionary since, because of new findings, additions are constantly being made to the thousands of words already known. The nearest to a comprehensive list is the famous Woerterbuch file in Berlin, on which the bulk of the work was completed by 1927. Since then, many words have been discovered, with new refinements continually being made to existing definitions by scholars.

Large strides have been made since World War II in Egyptology, and this progress still continues. Many new objects were unearthed during the rush in archaeological digging prior to the flooding of Upper Nile sites by the waters of the high Aswan Dam. Study of the hieroglyphs on these discoveries and other objects goes on daily.

Of the words given in this list, many can be recognized on monuments, statues, and texts you will encounter while reading books illustrating Egyptian objects, or visiting museums. The pronunciation shown after the English word is the nearest equivalent possible when using English language associations only. For closer approximation of the sounds, the scientific notation is also given. To use this method, refer to the alphabetical list on page 14. It is recommended that the method of the Egyptologists be learned and used, if you have a choice of using either system of vocalization.

Good scribes had an extensive vocabulary

accurate		bald
a-ka ꜥḳꜣ		wesh wš
alert		bed
medes mds		henkit ḥnkyt
answer, *verb*		bend
wesheb wšb		waf wꜥf
approach someone, to		beneficial, to be
khen ḫn		akh ꜣḫ
axe		bite, *verb & noun*
mi-neb mỉnb		peseh psḥ
bad, be		blood
djoo ḏw		senef snf
baker		boat
reteh-ty rtḥty		depet dpt

bow down, to kesi *ksỉ*		child khered *ḫrd*	
box hen *ḥn*		clothe, to djeba *ḏbꜣ*	
break open negi *ngỉ*		collect, to sak *sꜣḳ*	
breathe neshep *nšp*		come, to yoo *ỉw*	
bring, to ini *ỉnỉ*		command, to sha *šꜣ*	
bring mes *ms*		complaint yoo *ỉw*	
burn, to neser *nsr*		cup henet *ḥnt*	
bury, to qeres *ḳrs*		cut off, to hesek *ḥsḳ*	
capture, verb & noun kefa *kfꜥ*		damage, to neken *nkn*	
cat mi-ew *mỉw*		dance, to ib *ỉb*	
celebrate, feast hetes *ḥts*		darkness kekooee *kkw(y)*	
chair hetmet *ḥtmt*		defend nekh *nḫ*	
change, to shebi *šbỉ*		descend hai *hꜣỉ*	
chief, head tep *tp*		desert meroo *mrw*	

desire, to abi *ȝbi*		eye iret *irt*	
detain ihem *iḥm*		face her *ḥr*	
dispatch, letter shat *šɛt*		fat ad *ɛd*	
dog yoo *iw*		family mehwet *mḥwt*	
door seba *sbȝ*		feet redwee *rdwy*	
embrace, verb & noun hepet *ḥpt*		few nehee *nhy*	
empty shooi *šwi*		fire, flame sedjet *sḏt*	
enter ak *ɛḳ*		fish, noun rem *rm*	
err, to nenem *nnm*		flee wetekh *wtḫ*	
evening meshroo *mšrw*		flower hereret *ḥrrt*	
every, all, any neb *nb*		fly, to pa *pȝ*	
evil khoo-oo *ḫww*		follow, to shemes *šms*	
excellent, be iker *iḳr*		food shaboo *šȝbw*	
exist, be wenen *wnn*		foot red *rd*	

freeze
   hes *ḥs*
		hear, obey, noun
		   sedjem *sḏm*	

friend(s)
   mer *mr*
		high, to be
		   kai *ḳȝi*	

front
   hat *ḥȝt*
		horizon
		   akhet *ȝḫt*	

garden
   hesep *ḥsp*
		horse
		   sesmet *ssmt*	

go
   shem *šm*
		hot, be
		   shemem *šmm*	

gracious, be
   yam *iȝm*
		house
		   hoot *ḥwt*	

great, be
   aai *ʿȝi*
		hungry, be
		   heker *ḥḳr*	

greed, be greedy
   afa *ȝfʿ*
		idle, be
		   wesef *wsf*	

guard
   saoo *sȝw*
		illness
		   shenoo *šnw*	

guilty, be
   kheben *ḫbn*
		in
		   em *m*	

hail, call
   hee *hy*
		irrigate, to
		   netef *ntf*	

hair
   shenee *šny*
		is
		   yoo *iw*	

happen
   sep *sp*
		jubilation
		   ihehee *iḥḥy*	

hasten
   khakh *ḫȝḫ*
		jug for water
		   nemset *nmst*	

Patience and a good memory are useful qualities when improving your vocabulary

kiss, to
  sen *sn*

lasso, to
  sepeh *spḥ*

laugh
  sebetj *sbṯ*

law
  hep *ḥp*

lead, guide
  seshem *sšm*

leg
  sebek *sbḳ*

linger
  sai *sꜣỉ*

many
  asha *ꜥšꜣ*

measure, to
  khai *ḫꜣỉ*

men
  rehoo *rḥw*

milk
  yatet *ỉꜣtt*

monkey
  kee *ky*

month abed *ꜣbd*		old, be yaooee *iꜣwi*	
morning dooa *dwꜣ*		open, to sen *sn*	
mother moot *mwt*		overthrow petekh *ptḥ*	
mountain djoo *ḏw*		pain ahoo *ꜣhw*	
mouse penoo *pnw*		palace ah *ꜥḥ*	
neck nehbet *nḥbt*		papyrus scroll shefdoo *šfdw*	
need sar *sꜣr*		perfume, ointment newed *nwd*	
neighbors henoo *hnw*		perish, destroy seki *ski*	
north mehet *mḥt*		pig reri *rri*	
not know, to khem *ḥm*		ponder wawa *wꜣwꜣ*	
number rekhet *rḥt*		praise sensee *sns(y)*	
nurse mena *mnꜥ*		prince ireepat *r-pꜥt*	
oar hepet *ḥpt*		punish hed *ḥd*	
official ser *sr*		quiet, noun seger *sgr*	

rage, verb & noun neshnee *nšny*		save nedj *nḏ*	
require, demand wekha *wḫꜣ*		say, to djed *ḏd*	
retreat kheti *ḫti*		scratch, to akha *ꜣḫꜥ*	
reward, verb & noun feka *fkꜣ*		secret, to be sheta *štꜣ*	
rich, be khewed *ḫwd*		send, to hab *hꜣb*	
robber awai *ꜥwꜣi*		shave, to khak *ḫꜥḳ*	
rob, to hootef *ḥwtf*		short, be hooa *ḥwꜥ*	
roof, ceiling hat *hꜣt*		silent, be ger *gr*	
row (a boat) kheni *ḫni*		sink, submerge herep *hrp*	
run, to gesi *gsi*		sit, dwell hemsi *ḥmsi*	
sadness hat-ib *hꜣt-ib*		sky pet *pt*	
sail, to hetaoo *ḥtꜣw*		slaughter khaeet *ḫꜣyt*	
salt hemat *ḥmꜣt*		sleep, to keded *ḳdd*	
sand shaee *šꜥy*		smash, destroy seseh *ssḥ*	

sniff tepi *tpi*		sword sefet *sft*	
son sa *si*		talk, discuss wefa *wfi*	
sorrow ianoo *irnw*		taste, to dep *dp*	
stairway rewed *rwd*		teach, to seba *sbi*	
stand, arise aha *rhr*		thief itja *iti*	
star seba *sbi*		this pen *pn*	
statue (of woman) repeet *rpyt*		time, period rek *rk*	
stick, rod iaat *iiit*		to en *n*	
stop ab *ib*		tooth ibeh *ibḥ*	
strength pehtee *pḥty*		tree shen *šn*	
strike, beat hee-ee *ḥii*		turn backwards mesneh *msnḥ*	
strong, be nekhet *nḫt*		unite sma *smi*	
surround sheni *šni*		upper part heroo *ḥrw*	
swallow, to sedeb *sdb*		upside down, be sekhed *sḫd*	

Well-chosen words were important in praying for a good life after death

valley
  inet *int*
		where?
		  tjen *ṯn*	

walk, to
  sootoot *swtwt*
		who? what? which?
		  see *sy*	

wash, to
  iai *ỉꜥỉ*
		who, which
		  entee *nty*	

water
  moo *mw*
		wife, woman
		  hemet *ḥmt*	

weak
  fen *fn*
		wood, stick
		  khet *ḫt*	

weapons
  khaoo *ḫꜥw*
		write
		  sesh *sš*	

wisdom
  saret *sꜣrt*
		wrong, noun
		  nef *nf*	

wish, noun
  ib *ỉb*
		yesterday
		  sef *sf*	

Most hieroglyphs that remain were for funerary, religious or official use

TYPICAL SENTENCES

Here are some typical hieroglyphic sentences. Three lines are given for each:

1. *The hieroglyphs.* The examples shown actually exist, taken from ancient Egyptian texts.

2. *The sounds.* As near as can be achieved with standard English characters, the pronunciation of the Egyptian words is given. The alphabetical table on page 14 gives additional information about sounding of the words according to the pronunciation of professional Egyptologists.

3. *English translation.* The English and the equivalent Egyptian word are related by number. Occasionally slight modifications in the English words are needed to make the translation colloquially satisfactory. Note that the grammatical structure in the two languages is often inverted, or requires words to be added in English that were merely implied in the Egyptian.

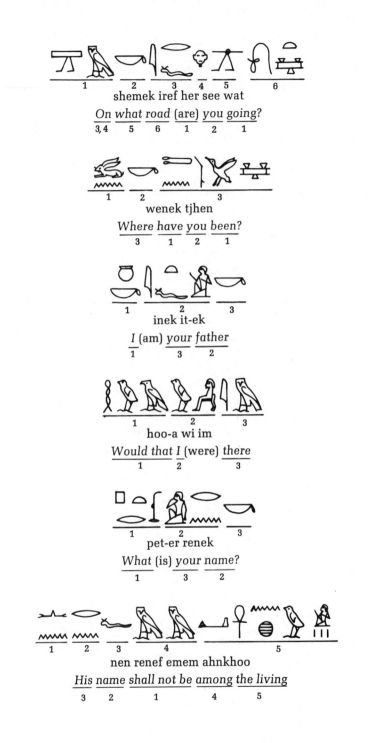

shemek iref her see wat

On what road (are) you going?
3, 4   5   6   1   2   1

wenek tjhen

Where have you been?
3   1   2   1

inek it-ek

I (am) your father
1   3   2

hoo-a wi im

Would that I (were) there
1   2   3

pet-er renek

What (is) your name?
1   3   2

nen renef emem ahnkhoo

His name shall not be among the living
3   2   1   4   5

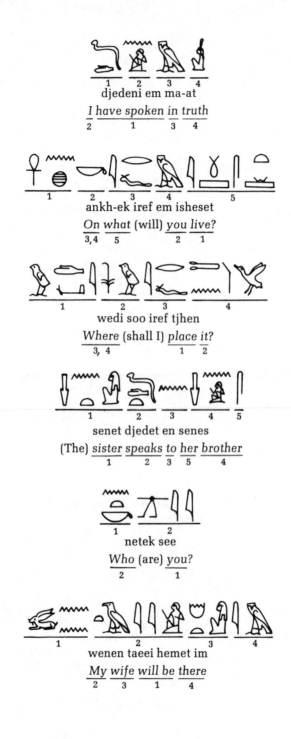

djedeni em ma-at

I have spoken in truth
2   1   3 4

ankh-ek iref em isheset

On what (will) you live?
3,4   5   2 1

wedi soo iref tjhen

Where (shall I) place it?
3, 4   1 2

senet djedet en senes

(The) *sister speaks to her brother*
1   2   3 5   4

netek see

Who (are) *you?*
2   1

wenen taeei hemet im

My wife will be there
2   3   1   4

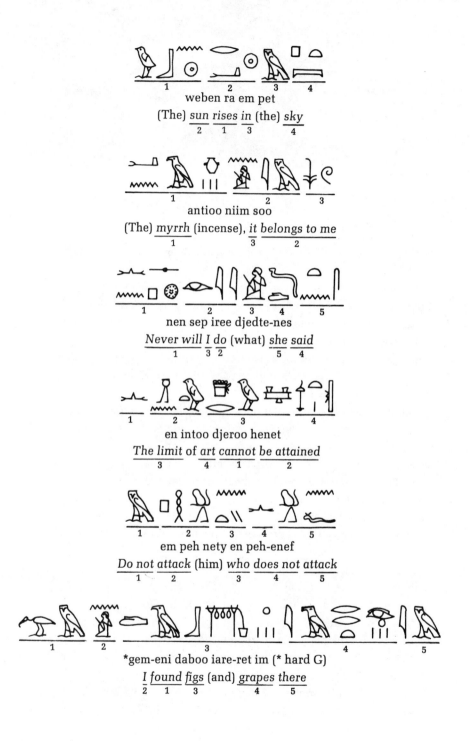

weben ra em pet

(The) <u>sun</u> <u>rises</u> <u>in</u> (the) <u>sky</u>
   2   1   3   4

antioo niim soo

(The) <u>myrrh</u> (incense), <u>it</u> <u>belongs to</u> <u>me</u>
     1   3   2

nen sep iree djedte-nes

<u>Never will</u> <u>I</u> <u>do</u> (what) <u>she</u> <u>said</u>
     1   3 2   5   4

en intoo djeroo henet

<u>The</u> <u>limit</u> of <u>art</u> <u>cannot</u> <u>be attained</u>
   3   4   1   2

em peh nety en peh-enef

<u>Do not</u> <u>attack</u> (him) <u>who</u> <u>does not</u> <u>attack</u>
 1   2   3   4   5

gem-eni daboo iare-ret im (hard G)

<u>I</u> <u>found</u> <u>figs</u> (and) <u>grapes</u> <u>there</u>
 2   1   3   4   5

The Egyptians had to know their grammar well before carving . . . mistakes were not easily corrected!

GRAMMAR

If you find a sense of achievement in mastering grammar and syntax, there is ample opportunity for enjoying yourself in the study of hieroglyphs. The ancient Egyptians evolved a spoken and written language which was remarkably advanced. It has been extensively analyzed, and books are available to assist you in exploring the subject as far as you want to go. Typical examples of what you will learn in a study of grammar include the following:

There are two genders of nouns, masculine and feminine. Feminine words end with a *t* ⌒ . Nouns not terminating with a *t* are masculine.

Most sentences begin with a verb, such as *ran, love,* or *wish.* The next word is the subject, or person performing the action, as: I, you, it, boat, man. This is followed by the person or object receiving the action, or about which the action is centered. These are verbal sentences, the normal word order being (1) verb, (2) subject, (3) object. There is a wide variety of other types of sentences and phrases, each having its own rules of construction.

When speaking of one or more persons, use one of three classes of endings: singular, dual, or plural. To show two of something, *wy* is added to the word, which is masculine. If it were a feminine word, *ty* ⎯ would be added. To make a word plural, add three vertical strokes to the *w* , and place them at the end of a masculine word. For a feminine word, add the same three vertical strokes to a *t* , which is used to end the word.

There is difficulty in making tenses clear. The Middle Egyptian period, upon which much of the grammar is based, probably had spoken indications for giving a time element as to past, present, or future. However, this is missing in the written hieroglyphs.

When expressing a negative idea, or saying something did not exist or occur, the word of negation comes first in the sentence, or the clause being negated.

PRONOUNS

To give a somewhat extended view of Egyptian grammar, consider the pronouns. There are several classes. Their application depends on their use. For example, the "suffix pronouns" are placed after the verb, as follows:

SINGULAR		PLURAL
𓀀 I, me, my	*First Person*	We, us, our 𓈖
𓂝 Thou, thee, you (masculine)	*Second Person*	You, your (both masc. & fem.) 𓈖
𓏏 Thou, thee, you (feminine)		
𓆑 He, him, his, it (masculine)	*Third Person*	They, them, their 𓏏 𓈖 (masc. & fem.)
𓊃 She, her, it (feminine)		

These pronouns are used to show possessions, such as "*his* ear," "*their* city," "*her* daughter." They are used after a preposition, such as "*to* me," or "*with* her." Also, suffix pronouns are used to indicate the person performing the action, such as "*thou* sayest" or "*she* hears."

Another class of allied words, the dependent pronouns, are employed as the object of a verb, or as the subject after an adjectival predicate. Examples are, "He sends *him*" and "Unhappy art *thou* with me."

The other major type, independent pronouns, occurs almost always at the beginning of a sentence, and indicates the person about whom the speaking is done. "*He* is thy father," "*Thou* art my master," "*I* am good." Grammar text books expand on the full usage of these pronouns, as well as on other elements of the language's construction and usage. There exist, of course, many additional rules of grammar beyond those mentioned.

The Egyptian story of Creation is depicted by the arched body of Nut, representing the sky, held up by Geb, the Earth god

THE CALENDAR

The Egyptians found, during prehistoric times, that besides eventual departure from present earthly life, one thing was certain—the Nile River would rise to flood stage beginning approximately each 365th day. Therefore they created a year divided into 12 months of 30 days each, to which were added five extra days, to make 365. This became the civil year, and was used for calendar as well as dating purposes. New Year's day, "the opening of the year," was Ⓤ, or "wepet renpet."

At one time it was noticed that, just before flooding began each year, the star Sirius would become visible in the sky shortly before sunrise. This would be about July 19th on the present Julian calendar. The time became identified as ⚏ ∆ ✶ "peret sepdet," the "going up of the goddess Sothis." This began the Egyptian astronomical year.

But an error was creeping into the calendar. Allowance was not made for the fact that the year is actually 365¼ days long. Due to the quarter-day difference between the civil calendar of 365 days and the Sothis cycle, the civil calendar gradually pulled ahead by one day each four years. In 40 years, the civil calendar was 10 days ahead, and in 400 years the calendars were about 100 days apart. At this rate of ¼ day each 365 days, it would take 1,460 years for the two years to coincide again. Actually it was 1,456 years. Therefore, on the civil calendar, the inundation of the Nile sometimes occurred in the winter, other times in the summer, autumn, or spring. Corrections to the present Julian calendar, such as the addition of Leap Years, now avoid the problem.

ḥɜt-sp 2 ɜbd 3(n) ɜḫt sw 1, ḥr ḥm n n-sw-bɜt N-mɜˁt-Rˁ

Year 2, third month of inundation, day one under
the Majesty of King Nema-re (Ammenemes III)

Nevertheless, to measure high or low periods of the Nile, three seasons of the year were recognized and named: 1—The Season of the Inundation; 2—The Winter, or emergence of the fields from the water; and 3—Summer, or the dry period. The true New Year's day was therefore "First Month of Inundation, Day 1":

At no time throughout the period of the Pharaohs were the years numbered continuously. The Egyptians dated their inscriptions according to the years of their Pharaohs' reigns. In the earlier dynasties, each year was named after an important event, such as "the year of the census," "the year of the fighting," and so forth. In the Old and Middle Kingdom, the rulers also dated periods according to their years on the throne.

The Egyptians were the first to divide the day into 24 hours. Of the 24 hours, 12 hours were for the day and 12 for the night. Each hour had its own religious or practical name. There were no precise instruments for measuring the hours. In summertime, the hours of the day were longer than those of the wintertime. Hours received such names as "the time of the perfume of the mouth (midday meal)," "supper hour," and "time-of-night hour." To write "fourth hour of night," instead of a designation such as 10 P.M., the Egyptian would say:

Lastly, the Egyptians divided the year into decans, or tens, giving identification to every 10-day period. Each was recognized because it was measured by the rising of a particular constellation during the night when the decan was due. This divided the year into 36 parts. Present-day astrologers still employ the same system, originated so long ago.

Fragment of the Rhind Mathematical Papyrus in hieratic script

NUMBERS

Of all the ways the Egyptians could have developed a system of numbers, it is interesting to note that theirs was in multiples of 10. It is a system which time has proved to be the most practical for everyday use, even after 5,000 years of employment.

Seven signs were used for designating numbers:

1 | 10 ∩   100 ❟   1,000 ⚱   10,000 ⌡   100,000 ⌐   1,000,000 ⚓

Numbers using these symbols, might be: 75 ∩∩∩∩| | | or 614 ⟨⟨⟨ ∩ | | | |

Notice that the higher values are written before the lower ones. When any of the figures is a multiple of any of the basic numbers, they are repeated as many times as necessary.

When it comes to fractions, the most common method of expression was to write an *r* ⬭. Anything placed below or alongside it was that fractional part. Therefore ⬭ equals 1/5th. To write 1/360th, the signs were: ⟨⟨⟨ ∩∩∩

Fractions which have more than "1" in the top portion brought about a different situation. In 3/7ths, for example, several fractions are linked together. Thus 3/7ths would be noted as being 1/4 + 1/7 + 1/28, which is equal to 7/28 + 4/28 + 1/28, or 3/7ths.

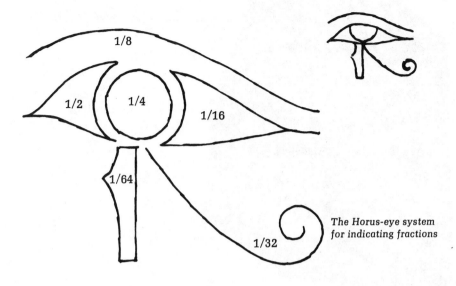

The Horus-eye system for indicating fractions

In one actual document, the Rhind papyrus of about 1600 B.C., 2/61 was written as 1/40 + 1/244 + 1/488 + 1/610. Cumbersome as this method seems, the Greeks and Romans were burdened with the same complexity in their own fractional measures.

When measuring grain or land, the ancient people of the Nile used a more primitive type of fraction, associated with dividing numbers in half. The grain measure is based on the eye of the god Horus, whose pictorial representation was that of a hawk. Each part of the eye represented a fraction. See above.

These fractions were generally added together to measure quantities, and on occasion were intermixed with the previously described fractions. The Horus fractions came into use after 1200 B. C. They are found in the hieratic script writing, rather than hieroglyphs, where only the ½ is found.

Dimensions were in a measure that in English is identified as "cubits," a term used so frequently in the Bible. The cubit's size was based on the distance from elbow to fingertips, averaging about 20.64″ long. Every cubit was divided into seven parts, each of those sections being a "palm." Palms were divided into four digits. The palm was about 3″ wide, and the digit about the thickness of a finger, or 3/4″.

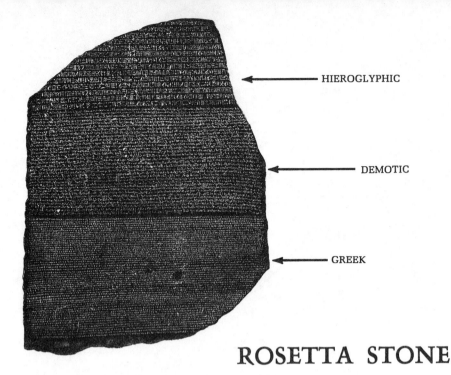

HIEROGLYPHIC

DEMOTIC

GREEK

ROSETTA STONE

It was July, 1799. The invading army of Napoleon was digging in for a long stay, after its conquest of Egypt. One of the sites selected for fortification was the old Mameluke ruins of Fort Rashid in the delta region of the Nile. The foundations were to be extended, and a new Fort Julian erected on them. Nearby, at Rosetta, a branch of the Nile could be used for bringing in supplies from the Mediterranean.

As the French soldiers dug, they came across a black basalt stone which seemed quite unusual in that three different styles of writing were carved into the surface. The engineering officer, Pierre Francois Xavier Bouchard, realizing that the stone might have more significance than first met the eye, reported its discovery to his commander, General Manou, who in turn ordered it to be brought to Alexandria. Gradually the realization began to grow that the three forms of writing might actually say the same thing, so that knowledge of one language would give clues to the unknown features of the other two. It remained to see if this theory were true.

Napoleon was shown the writing. He was so impressed by the carvings that he brought two printers from Paris to Cairo, just to pull proof copies. They inked the stone, placed paper on it, and rubbed. Good impressions resulted. These were sent to scholars in many parts of Europe, so that they could be studied.

Meanwhile, as the proofs underwent a long period of examination, the French fortunes waned in Egypt. By 1801 the English forces had defeated them, and in the surrender, the Rosetta Stone passed to the victor's hands. In due course the stone was transported to the British Museum in London, where it still holds an honored position for all visitors to see.

This ancient stone is 3'9" high, 2'4½" wide, and 11" thick. It is but part of a larger piece, estimated to have been five or six feet high originally. The missing parts have never been found.

On the Rosetta Stone are two languages, Greek and Egyptian. The Egyptian portion is written in two forms:

A. *Hieroglyphic.* This is topmost of the writings. This writing style was used throughout Egyptian history for nearly all documents and monuments intended for public viewing where the mantle of formal presentation was desirable. This type of writing corresponds to our present printing, particularly where Old English letters might be used to make the document or wording seem especially impressive.

B. *Demotic.* This was the middle group, being a highly abbreviated "handwritten" form of the hieroglyphs. Actually, this was the principal and popular writing form of the time when the stone was carved.

C. *Greek.* This was the language shown at the bottom. Therefore the implication of the writing was that the stone was carved after the arrival of Alexander the Great in 332 B.C.

Since a large section of the stone was missing, the problem of finding the matching portions of the three scripts that said the same thing was all the more difficult. Most of the Greek text and all of the demotic were preserved, but a large portion of the hieroglyphic text was absent. Therefore when the scholars worked to translate the stone and decipher the languages, they worked mainly from the demotic and Greek-letter portions.

That the job was eventually done successfully attests to the hard work and skill of the scholars. A large portion of the missing hieroglyphic text was found in a duplicate monument in 1898, and on a copy of the text carved on a temple wall at Philae, now underwater behind the Aswan Dam.

Scarab or dung beetle.
Triliteral for "bring
to pass; to become."
Pronounced "kheper"

THE DECIPHERERS

When copies of the Rosetta Stone texts reached Europe, scholars went to work on it immediately. The Greek text was translated by 1802. Results from the first studies of the demotic portion were achieved the same year by Akerblad, a Swedish diplomat. He identified all of the proper names in the demotic section which occurred in the Greek section, plus a few other words. All of these were written alphabetically. Brilliant as was his work, it led him to the assumption that the rest of the demotic text was alphabetic. This was to prove in error, but it would take 12 years before the erroneous premise was set aside. The mistaken assumption also existed that some of the signs were vowels, which caused other false starts.

It was not until 1814 that the scientist Thomas Young deduced that the demotic writing was not entirely alphabetic. By 1816 he had developed a vocabulary of 86 words associating the Greek with the demotic. He then found that the groups of hieroglyphs with ovals around them, or cartouches as they are better known, contain royal names. Using several hieroglyphic texts, he recognized the names of Cleopatra and Berenice, and that of Ptolemy.

This breakthrough by Young helped pave the way for the work of Jean Francois Champollion of France, who had been laboring independently on the decipherment and was coming to similar conclusions. By the time he had reached the year of his death in 1832, Champollion had corrected and greatly enlarged Young's list of hieroglyphs, and deciphered the names and titles of most of the Roman emperors who had ruled Egypt. He also formulated a system for understanding the Egyptian grammar and evolved a method of decipherment which became the

Jean François Champollion

foundation for all the later progress by Egyptologists in the study of hieroglyphs.

Although the Rosetta Stone showed the way to interpreting the royal names in the hieroglyphs and obtaining the phonetic equivalent of many signs, the language could not have been understood without a knowledge of Coptic. This late stage of the ancient Egyptian language using Greek letters and a few signs derived from demotic, was in a language that had never been lost. The Copts used their much-changed version of the ancient Egyptian language, employing Greek script, for translations of the Bible, liturgies, and other writings of Christianity. Champollion realized the importance of knowing Coptic if he were ever to understand the hieroglyphs, and as a result he had learned the language as a youth. His work enabled him to achieve the success which made him famous, when he bridged the gap between the Greek letters and the uninterpreted hieroglyphs.

The work of Champollion was but a small beginning. In the next hundred years the knowledge of Egyptian writing was immensely broadened. A tremendous amount was achieved by the 1920's. In 1927, compilation was completed on an exhaustive file of 1½ million reference slips by scholars throughout the world, begun in 1897. It formed a collection of all words in all the known Egyptian inscriptions and manuscripts, the file being the Berlin Woerterbuch. This material is being gradually brought together in a series of books, and the work is still in progress. Many words have been added since 1927. An additional index was published in 1963, supplementing the volumes already produced.

Top portion of Rosetta Stone.
Ptolemy cartouche, shown above
and on following pages, is
reversed to simplify reading

SOLVING THE MYSTERY

Thomas Young reached the conclusion in 1814 that the oval or cartouche marks surrounding some of the hieroglyphs contained royal names. He noted that one name in the Greek portion of the Rosetta Stone, Ptolemy or Ptolemaios, was repeated six times. Because the stone surface had been chiselled when the Greek language was employed in Egypt, Young started with the assumption that the writing inside the cartouches could be the same name, in hieroglyphs.

In 1815 an obelisk was found at Philae on the Nile River which also contained both Greek and Egyptian writing. On the monument, the name "Cleopatra" appeared in Greek. It was therefore assumed that in the cartouche in Egyptian on this stone it was the same name, Cleopatra, repeated in hieroglyphs. The problem was to prove it.

On Philae obelisk

Assisting Young in his search were the Greek words, which Young could read: "This decree is to be set up on a stela of hard stone, in sacred, native and Greek letters." Consequently Young went on the assumption made right along, that the two Egyptian scripts were either actual translations or paraphrased versions of the Greek text.

On the Philae obelisk they also had a cartouche which was almost the same as the one on the Rosetta Stone. Young started with the assumption it was "Ptolemy":

On Philae obelisk

On Rosetta Stone (repeated six times with slight changes)

Placing the Ptolemy cartouche above Cleopatra's, and numbering the signs, Ptolemy 1 matches Cleopatra 5:

Ptolemy

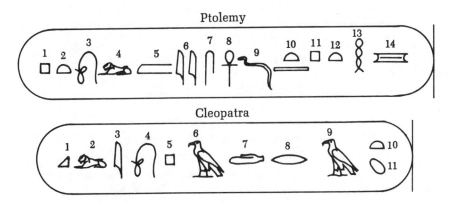

Cleopatra

Since Ptolemy starts with a P, assume that □ is P.

The second letter in Cleopatra ✐ is the same as Ptolemy 4. Based on the sounds of both names, the implication is strong that the sign is an L. If this is so, then Cleopatra 1 would be a hard-sounding C, or a K. Now substituting letters for pictures, this much is known:

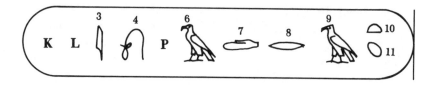

If the Egyptians pronounced Cleopatra the same way as at present, they would need an equivalent for an "e" and an "o," as the third and fourth letters, in between the L and the P. As an experiment, assume that Number 3 character ⧘ is an E, and Number 4 ⧘ is an O.

In cartouches of Cleopatra found elsewhere, the pictures were the same as shown except for Number 7, in which △ was often used instead of ◠. The assumption would be that these are either the same or fairly similar. The △ occurs as Number 2 in Ptolemy. Therefore it might be worth trying a T in position Number 7 of the Cleopatra cartouche.

In Cleopatra, Numbers 6 and 9 are identical. Because "A" seems to fit logically at these positions, a hawk 𓅊 can tentatively be assumed to represent the sound of an A.

Substituting the letters deciphered thus far, the cartouche would be:

$$\text{K} \quad \text{L} \quad \text{E} \quad \text{O} \quad \text{P} \quad \text{A} \quad \text{T} \quad \underset{8}{\text{◠}} \quad \text{A} \quad \underset{10}{\text{△}} \quad \underset{11}{\text{○}}$$

It was Thomas Young who noticed that when the name of a goddess, queen, or princess was mentioned, two signs were placed at the end of the name ⧖. This being so, the characters would not necessarily have to be pronounced, but would act as determinatives to show that the person described is feminine.

The final picture, Number 8 ◠, must, by implication, be an "R." The name CLEOPATRA is therefore spelled out in hieroglyphs.

Substitute the known letters in the Ptolemy cartouche:

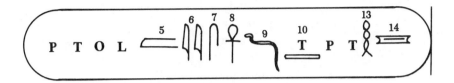

Immediately it becomes clear that there is more in the oval than the name Ptolemy. Elsewhere the name is found carved as follows:

Therefore the additional part of the name fits the Greek text on the Rosetta Stone, meaning "long-lived, beloved of Ptah."

Letter Number 5, by deduction, seems to represent M, and Number 6 would be an I or Y. The Greek name of Ptolemy is Ptolemaios. The remaining deduction, then, would indicate that ⎮ is an S.

These values were soon applied to another name found elsewhere:

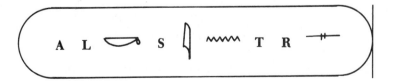

Substituting the letters already deciphered, the cartouche could be interpreted thus far:

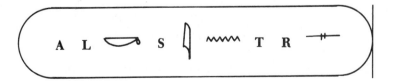

It was already known, from the early efforts of Young, that was an N, discovered when the name of Berenice was analyzed, she having followed Ptolemy I as ruler. It was deduced that the last symbol— —was an S, since most Greek names end in this fashion, and the cartouche had been found among Greek writing too.

It was also found that some of the cartouches of Cleopatra began with a , giving the implication that the sign had a C or K sound. The name in the hieroglyphs thus far would be:

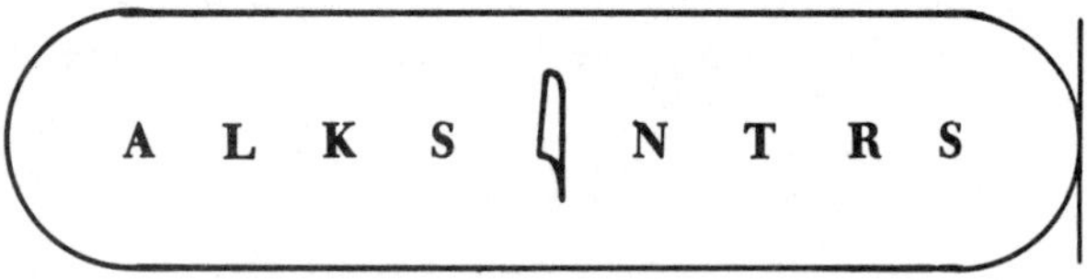

The name is the Egyptian spelling and pronunciation of Alexandros, or Alexander of Macedonia, to whom Egypt yielded without resistance in 332 B. C. The remaining would therefore be either an E or A.

Through following the same line of reasoning, and using the signs already known, the rest of the Egyptian hieroglyphs became known to scholars, clearing away more than 1,500 years of mystery about one of the earliest written languages in the history of mankind.

WHAT THE STONE SAYS

In the ninth year of the reign of Ptolemy V, Epiphanes by name, a decree was passed by the General Council of Egyptian priests. They were meeting at Memphis to commemorate the anniversary of the coronation of Ptolemy V as king of all Egypt. The year was 196 B.C. The stone notes the occasion, first giving the date, and then publishing a series of epithets which proclaimed the devotion of the king to the gods, and his love for the Egyptians.

Ptolemy V was, of course, of Greek heritage. After Alexander the

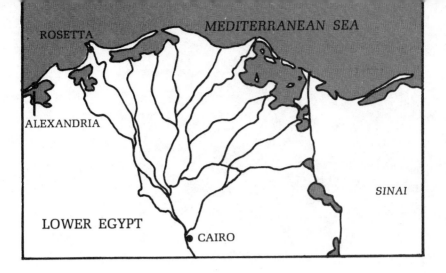

Great had brought Egypt under his rule in 332 B.C., and later died at Babylon on his return from the expedition to India, his generals divided the lands of the Macedonian into several parts, of which Ptolemy took Egypt. In theory, the various generals were to rule in the name of the mentally incompetent half-brother of Alexander, Philip Arridaeus, and Alexander's posthumously-born son, the infant Alexander. These two kings were murdered in the wars between Alexander's successors, at which time Ptolemy dropped the pretense that he was ruling in their name and proclaimed himself King of Egypt.

His progeny remained in Egypt and retained the ru.ership. Among the descendants was the famous line of seven Cleopatras. The seventh Cleopatra was the glamorous queen associated with Marc Antony and Julius Caesar in history and in literature.

The second section of the inscription on the Rosetta Stone listed 17 benefits that Pharaoh Ptolemy V had conferred on Egypt. Included were gifts to the temples, forgiveness of debts, the release of prisoners, reduction of taxes, the sending of troops against Egypt's enemies, and restoration of sacred buildings.

In gratitude, according to the stone, the priests decided to put statues of Ptolemy in every temple, create a new holiday for him, and make shrines to him to be loaned to private individuals for their homes and for carrying in processions. It was also ordered that copies of the decree be set up in "all temples of the first second, and third orders." That is why one copy of the decree was found at Rosetta, and other copies of the text have since been found at different locations in Egypt.

*A student's practice
of hieratic script
on his copyboard*

FORMS OF WRITING

HIERATIC

To speed the writing of hieroglyphs, a form of handwriting was developed concurrently with them. It was used from the beginning of Egyptian writing, particularly on non-monumental applications. Employing reeds and brushes in writing made it easiest to form marks which simulated the hieroglyphs, rather than trying to duplicate them in full.

Although the two writing forms appear at first glance to be quite different, there are strong relationships. For a quick comparison of likenesses, look at the handwritten script and the printed alphabetic characters of any modern western language.

The name "hieratic" was quite late in origin, even though the script to which it applied had been in use for about 3,000 years. Since the priests in Egypt, after the arrival of the Greeks, were among the chief users of writing, the handwriting style came to be described as priestly, or based on the Greek word for this, "hieratikos."

By the XVIII Dynasty hieratic was found on almost all papyrus texts, including such religious uses as the Book of the Dead. By the XXI Dynasty it was used on stone carvings and in many more religious scripts. By the time of the Rosetta Stone in 196 B.C. hieratic had been supplanted by the more cursive demotic writing style.

Literary hieratic of the Twelfth Dynasty with
hieroglyphic equivalents written by a modern Egyptologist

Official hieratic of the Twentieth Dynasty with
hieroglyphic equivalents written by a modern Egyptologist

Literary demotic of the Third Century B.C., with
hieroglyphic equivalents written by a modern Egyptologist

A complaint and plea for assistance, in demotic script

DEMOTIC

Although hieratic was a simplified form of writing the hieroglyphs in script form, a more rapid style of writing began to predominate around 700 B.C. This was the "demotic" style, derived from the Greek word "demotikos," or popular. It continued in use until about 500 A.D.

COPTIC

After the Greek-speaking Macedonians took over Egypt in 332 B.C., the spoken language of the Nile nation began to change even more rapidly than before. Many Greek words came into everyday usage to supplement and supplant the Egyptian. In 30 B.C. following the battle of Actium in which the Roman, Octavian, defeated Antony and Cleopatra, Egypt became a Roman province. Further language changes occurred. The Greek word for Egypt had been "Aiguptos," the Roman word "Aegyptus." The Arabs, who arrived in 640 A.D., corrupted the name of the language they found in the country into the "Coptic" title now used, and the name of the people who used it into "Copts." Both were based on the Greek name.

The Coptic language and script developed, especially after 300 A.D., as the mode of expression by the Christian descendants of the ancient Egyptians. It is still used in some church services today, although little understood.

After the Arab conquest, Coptic was gradually replaced by Arabic. By 1500 A.D. it was virtually extinct, although its use lingered in small outlying areas and in isolated groups descended from the native Egyptians.

Coptic was written in the Greek alphabet, supplemented by seven characters based on demotic writing to write sounds occurring in Egyptian but not in Greek. The language is a very late stage of Egyptian, different in many ways from the older tongue of the early periods. Many Greek words appeared in the writing, and vowels of the Egyptian that were not written before now began to appear because Greek letters were used for language notation. Because of this, tenses became recognizable in writing. The normal changes of a fluid, dynamic language contributed to further changes.

Even though Coptic was a late development of the ancient Egyptian, with its many alterations, it is nevertheless a primary source for obtaining hints as to how the earlier hieroglyphs were vocalized. Therefore, although the use of Coptic as a key to the spoken language of early Egypt is not always accurate, it is still one of the best sources available.

*Coptic writing
on piece of pottery*

Heart and windpipe. Triliteral for good happy, beautiful. Pronounced "nefer"

CHANGING HIEROGLYPHS

Egypt had a culture which at first glance seems changeless and timeless. Actually, many conditions in the lives of the people were constantly being altered. Although there were art styles which seemed to freeze the modes of expression, and keep the hieroglyphic writings the same, the trained eye can note much change in many areas.

In the language, as already described, there were drastic changes even with Pharaonic Egypt, in addition to later alterations. Major forms of the written language are identified as Old Egyptian (Dynasties 1 through 10), Middle Egyptian (Dynasties 11 through 18), Late Egyptian (Dynasties 19 to 25), Demotic (Dynasties 26 to the beginning of the Christian era), and Coptic (from Christianity until Islam's influence).

Even though Egypt became an empire about 1500 B.C. and acquired some of the ways of other lands, its writings continued to be in the classical form for official and religious purposes. However, by the end of the XVIII Dynasty, starting with the Amarna period about 1370 B.C., alterations crept into the written language. These were based on contemporary popular expressions. Therefore the writing of the latter half of the New Kingdom period, in the XIX and XX Dynasties, no longer adhered fully to the classical form. However, the XXVI Dynasty, in which, rulership was from Sais in lower Egypt, 664 B.C. to 525 B.C., became a period of archaizing. In that time the Old Kingdom styles, motifs, forms, models, and language were deliberately sought and consciously imitated.

Despite the relatively static form of hieroglyphic writing which at first seems unchangeable, it is possible to date inscriptions by a careful

*Keeper of the grain,
grinding flour*

reading of the texts. Fixing of the time of writing might come from the spelling of various words, the grammatical sequence, the vocabulary, colloquialisms, archaeological relationship to other remains at the site, art styles, and other clues which the observer recognizes. Nevertheless, the changes that did occur were quite slow. A text of 700 B.C. may be found to have remarkably few alterations from the language of 2700 B.C., despite variations in the language of latter-day Egyptians. Slightly distorting this conclusion, of course, is the conscious attempt of the writers of 700 B.C. and shortly thereafter to try to copy Old Kingdom styles. Nevertheless, if you can read hieroglyphs of the XX Dynasty, you should do quite well at reading Old Kingdom hieroglyphs, of 1,500 years earlier. The same would not be true for a modern user of English reading Chaucer's works, unless he were especially trained.

As may be readily seen, the scribes were a conservative, tradition-loving group. Because of what they considered the sacredness of their picture-writing, and the importance which scribes held in the eyes of the average Egyptian, it is perhaps appropriate that the classical Egyptian hieroglyphic writings became known as "the words of the gods," or "the divine word," *medoo netjer:*

WHAT THEY WROTE ABOUT

What do the hieroglyphic, hieratic, and demotic writings say? The Egyptians wrote about everything that you might write about today. However, the ravages of time, carelessness, warfare, burial by drifting sands, and oxidation have obliterated the major portion of the materials on which the writing was done. Nevertheless, numerous tomb writings, wall carvings, papyrus scrolls, and other sources which contain writing still remain.

Some of the surviving papyrus manuscripts date back to the period between 2000 B.C. and 1000 B.C. This covers the time between the XII Dynasty and the XXI Dynasty. They contain remarkable ships' logs, ghost stories, poems, fables, hymns, love songs, and adventure stories. There are also documents on the subjects of medicine, mathematics, law, business, and worship.

In the Berlin Museum is the story of Sinuhe, an Egyptian in exile. His wanderings and adventures in Syria and Palestine are vividly recounted. In the Hermitage Museum of Leningrad is the story of a shipwrecked sailor who was washed up on the shores of a lonely island. There he has an exciting encounter with a golden snake.

The Orbiney Papyrus now in the British Museum dates back to 1220 B.C., telling a tale of jealousy, love, and hatred between two brothers and a wayward sister. In its earlier portion it parallels the Biblical story of Joseph and Potiphar's wife.

In the Brooklyn Museum is the Wilbour Papyrus, a record of land measurements and tax assessments during the fourth year of the reign of Ramses V, 1150 B.C.

The Papyrus Harris in London was the posthumously issued political testament of Ramses III, which contains a short historical section and grants of land as well as property to various temples. It was written probably by his successor, and was a fictional device whereby the successor gained the backing and stamp of legitimacy from the various temples in return for what was granted to them.

*Part of Chapter 168, "Offerings," in a XIX Dynasty
Book of the Dead papyrus entitled "Adoration of Osiris"*

Another document concerning Ramses III tells of a conspiracy among members of his harem and royal household. The papyrus describes the trial which followed, and what finally happened.

The Turin Canon of Kings, better known as the Turin King List, is the most important surviving document in the Egyptian language on the chronology of Egypt. Although written in the XIX Dynasty, it lists kings only up to the beginning of the XVIII Dynasty, or about 1567 B.C.

In the Great Medical Papyrus in Berlin, and the Ebers Papyrus formerly at Leipzig, the ancient Egyptian doctors described blood circulation, the functions of the heart and stomach, and parts of human anatomy. The Edwin Smith medical papyrus is a 16-foot roll about 3,600 years old, describing 48 surgical operations.

Such exceptional findings are in the minority, however. What remains, as the writings on statues, tomb walls, and coffins, is primarily for funerary, religious, and exaltation use. Since much knowledge of the ancient Egyptians has to be based on these, the problem is akin to archaeologists discovering your home town a few thousand years from now. Practically all books would have disintegrated. Knowledge of the language and people would be gained primarily from tombstones, build-

Alabaster canopic jars for vital organs. Heads represent the four compass directions, and the four sons of Horus

ing cornerstones, machine instruction plates, and statue inscriptions. The task of learning the language would be great, and to know of life in the 20th century in its true perspective would be herculean indeed!

That is the basic problem of learning about Egyptian life as it existed several thousand years ago. The bulk of the writing is concerned mainly with praising departed persons, offering prayers to the gods, or relaying instructions supposedly given by the deities.

The Pyramid Texts are the oldest Egyptian religious writings known, found on the walls of chambers in the kings' pyramids from the V Dynasty onward, or about 2400 B.C. Incantations are given in these inscriptions to please the gods and assure the dead Pharaoh of his rightful place and privileges in the sky. Rituals were also given, to be recited in connection with the daily offerings made at the temples.

The privilege of immortality belonged only to the king, by right, who could then grant its extension to whomever he might wish. However, in the First Intermediate Period, and in the Middle Kingdom, the concept of these kingly privileges had undergone a change. Death became more democratic, in the rights bestowed by it. Nobles used the wording formerly reserved for the Pharaohs' tombs only, so that the Pyramid Texts began to appear on the coffins of the noblemen and their families. Thus it was that the Pyramid Texts, with some alterations, additions, and omissions, were transformed into Coffin Texts.

Coffin Texts were those of non-royal persons, containing incantations to protect the deceased from thirst, hunger, and the many dangers of "the other world." However, since these non-royal people were feudal rulers of Egypt during the First Intermediate Period, they may have felt

Left to right, with contents:
Imset (man), *Holds liver*
Qebehsenuf (hawk). *Intestines*
Duamutef (jackal). *Stomach*
Hapi (ape). *Holds the lungs*

themselves entitled to usage of the sacred wording. To have a wooden coffin was expensive, and only the wealthy could afford it, which again fitted the nobility class.

About the time the New Kingdom began, the Coffin Texts underwent a transformation and became the Book of the Dead. This was basically the same collection of spells, incantations, and supplications to the gods, but again done with alterations, additions, and omissions. Now they were written on rolls of papyrus for insertion within the mummy case. The gloomy title, "Book of the Dead," was not given by the Egyptians, but by marauding Arabs of a much later time, since whenever they found the writing it was in the mummy cases. The Egyptians called the texts the "Book of Coming Forth by Day." It is not a book, but an assemblage of hymns to the gods Ra and Osiris, plus funerary spells.

Papyrus scrolls for the Book were relatively inexpensive in relation to an elaborate wooden coffin. Such a scroll could be a short book, or a long one, depending on the ability to pay. With the use of such papyrus scrolls, immortality and its privileges were now within the grasp of anyone who could afford it—not just the kings, royal families, and nobility.

Other texts of importance were also written on tomb walls, papyrus scrolls, coffins, and elsewhere. On the walls of New Kingdom Pharaohs are "The Book of What is in the Netherworld," "The Book of the Gates," and "The Book of the Caverns," which describes the topography of the netherworld. Other writings include the magical papyri giving magic spells and incantations for the protection from evil, or the casting of misfortune upon those who were thought to be deserving of it.

Akhnaton and Nefertiti

Name-defacing left Akhnaton statue like this

BRIEF ETERNITY

Ancient Egyptians believed that when a person's name was written, or carved in stone, the spirit could reside there forever after the individual had died. It was the pathway to life eternal. Destroy a person's name wherever it appeared, and he would no longer exist. His memory, and chance for eternal life, were obliterated. Even gods were subject to the same rule. Some odd twists occurred in Egyptian history pursuing this belief.

When Amenhotep IV became the Pharaoh in 1375 B.C., he faced a difficult problem. During his education while preparing for the throne, he had become convinced that there was an overall god, Aton, who deserved recognition as the sole god, rather than the many gods then worshiped. He naturally met opposition from the existing priesthood. Powerful followers of the sun god Amon were particularly opposed. The king had even been named after this same god. As normal methods of persuasion failed to win his way, the Pharaoh embarked on a complete annihilation of all existing gods.

Worship of the gods was banned. All priesthoods, including that of Amon, were dispossessed. Names of the gods were erased or destroyed wherever they appeared on monuments. In cemeteries the name of Amon was chiseled out of statues and tomb writings. Even the king's ancestors, including his father's memorials and statues, had references to gods deleted. Row upon row of the statues of deceased nobles had the gods' names destroyed. "Amon" ceased to exist, by official decree and action.

But what of the king's own name, Amenhotep? That had to go too. In honor of the newly declared god, Aton, the king changed his name to "Akhnaton." To get a fresh start, a new "Aton-city" was created, which became the capital of Egypt and domain for the god. For 17 years Akhnaton ruled. The rich and powerful old temples were either destroyed or vacated. The new state religion was enforced everywhere. Then Akhnaton died.

The old priesthoods, particularly of the Amonites, had been waiting for this day. All those years, their wrath was churning as they continued worshiping in secret. Military leaders were equally interested in a change, for their own reasons. When Tutankhaton eventually inherited the throne, political expediency and pressure forced him to let worship of Amon be reestablished. He even changed his name to Tutankhamon, in honor of the old sun god. Then, at age 18, he too died.

Haremhab in due course became Pharaoh. As Akhnaton's general, he had tried keeping the old priesthood contented, and the military too. Upon achieving the throne, he set about restoring order to the land, including reestablishing the old religions to their former prestige. Sculptors were sent throughout Egypt to continue restorations begun by Tutankhamon, putting back on monuments the names of gods which had been defaced by Akhnaton. At the same time, temples recently constructed to Aton were destroyed. Everywhere the name of Akhnaton was treated in the same way that he had treated the names of the gods. His tomb was wrecked, its reliefs chiselled out. His nobles' tombs were equally damaged. Every effort was made to erase all traces of his reign or existence in Egyptian history. His capital fell into disuse and destruction, the crumbled remains of which are now known as Tell el-Amarna. In effect, Akhnaton and the god Aton were never supposed to have existed, and they were certainly not given a way to attain a life eternal.

Fortunately for historical knowledge, these programs of destruction were not completely successful. Enough information remained so that much is known about these important parts of Egypt's past, throwing a light upon a section of history that was supposed to become a void.

Cartouche of Menes
(Narmer), I Dynasty

CARTOUCHE-READING

One of your earliest encounters with hieroglyph reading will probably come with efforts to decipher the name of an Egyptian Pharaoh. Here are suggestions which will help resolve questions bound to arise.

First, it is often difficult to recognize how far back in a text to begin reading, since each king had five names. Some of the Pharaohs' names could be quite lengthy. These five names had a fixed order of presentation, which assists the reader in identification of the king. It is generally by the fifth name that the pharaoh is known, or sometimes the fourth.

To Egyptologists, the fourth name is called the "prenomen," and the fifth the "nomen." Both of these were written in cartouches, while the other names were not: ◯〗

Cartouche is a French word meaning ornamental tablet upon which an inscription is, or can be, written. Although rarely shown, the fully drawn cartouche consists of two thicknesses of rope. These are tied together in such a way that the loose ends extend in a straight line, without the knot showing. In the ancient Egyptian language, this mark was called "snw," being from a verb-stem which means "to encircle." One interpretation is that the cartouche represents the king as "ruler of all that which is encircled by the sun."

The five names, in their correct sequence, are:

1. *The Horus name.* In Egyptian beliefs, the falcon-god Horus was reincarnated on earth in the form of the king. For this reason the god's identification as Horus was shown as part of his first name.

2. *Nebty name.* Pictured in a basket is Nekhbet, the vulture goddess of the Upper Egyptians, and in the other basket Edjo or Buto, the cobra-goddess of Lower Egypt. These two principal goddesses, or "ladies," represented their respective parts of Egypt. Incorporating them as part of the king's name showed that the ruler was king of both Upper Egypt

Ḥr ʿnḫ.mswt, nbty ʿnḫ mswt, Ḥr nbw ʿnḫ mswt, n-sw-bit
Ḫpr-kꜣ-Rʿ, sꜣ Rʿ S-n-Wsrt, dꜣ ʿnḫ ḏdt wꜣs mi Rʿ ḏt

Name of Sesostris I: Horus Life-of-Births, Two Ladies Life-of-Births, Horus of Gold
Life of Births, King of Upper and Lower Egypt being the spirit of Ra come into being,
Son of Ra Sesostris . . . the man of (the goddess) Wosret, (may he be) granted life,
stability and wealth like Ra, eternally

and Lower Egypt. Throughout dynastic history, the land was identified
as two regions, even when unified under one Pharaoh's rulership.

3. *Golden Horus name.* The third name affirms that the king is a
falcon or horus hawk made of gold. The full implication of its meaning
is not known for sure, even though there are numerous explanations.

4. *Nesewbity name.* The fourth name of the king is shown in a
cartouche following the title ✸ *n-sw-bit.* The word means "he who
belongs to the sedge and the bee." Again reference is made to the
Pharaoh as being "King of Upper and Lower Egypt," since the sedge
symbolizes Upper Egypt, and the bee Lower Egypt. Also in the fourth
name you will see ⊙,, representing the sun god Ra. The few cartouches
without it existed prior to Dynasty IX. Usage of Ra is akin to modern
Moslems all having Mohammed as their first name.

5. *The Family name.* Following ✸ *sꜣ* Ra, son of Ra, is the last name,
inside a cartouche. It was this name which was generally used by the
king before he gained the throne. For this reason it is the equivalent of
the present-day family name.

In reading the names in cartouches, patience is needed. Reference to
the gods is often combined with the name. Knowledge of some of the
possible names you might encounter will help in leading to proper
identification.

In spelling the names of Egyptian rulers, or in fact the name of any
inhabitant of ancient Egypt, you will probably encounter differences in
many books. Don't be too disturbed as to which is correct, since they
all may be right. It is the designation of the consonants that should be
similar. Vowels, which usually were added by peoples of a later era,
may be written as they believed the Egyptians might have pronounced
them. Numerous interpretations are therefore possible.

CHRONOLOGY OF EGYPT

Some dates overlap, due to separate rulership over divided portions of Egypt. The name shown with the dynasty number was the capital of the rulers during that dynasty. Most dates are from the Cambridge Ancient History series.

1. PREHISTORY   Up to 4000 B.C.

2. PRE-DYNASTIC PERIOD   4000-3100 B.C.

3. EARLY DYNASTIC PERIOD

   Dynasty I (Thinis)   3100-2890 B.C.
   Dynasty II (Thinis)   2890-2686 B.C.

4. OLD KINGDOM

   Dynasty III (Memphis)   2686-2613 B.C.
   Dynasty IV (Memphis)   2613-2494 B.C.
   Dynasty V (Memphis)   2494-2345 B.C.
   Dynasty VI (Memphis)   2345-2181 B.C.

5. FIRST INTERMEDIATE PERIOD

   Dynasty VII (Memphis)   2181-2173 B.C.
   Dynasty VIII (Memphis)   2173-2160 B.C.
   Dynasty IX (Herakleopolis)   2160-2130 B.C.
   Dynasty X (Herakleopolis) Lower Egypt   2130-2040 B.C.

6. MIDDLE KINGDOM

   Dynasty XI (Thebes) Upper Egypt   2133-1991 B.C.
   Dynasty XII (Thebes)   1991-1786 B.C.
   Dynasty XIII (Thebes)   1786-1633 B.C.

7. SECOND INTERMEDIATE PERIOD

   Dynasty XIV (Xois)   1786-1603 B.C.
   Dynasty XV (Hyksos Period)   1674-1567 B.C.
   Dynasty XVI (Hyksos Period)   1684-1567 B.C.
   Dynasty XVII (Thebes)   1650-1567 B.C.

A ship's mast. This triliteral means "to stand." Pronounced "aha"

8. NEW KINGDOM

Dynasty XVIII (Thebes)	1567-1320 B.C.
Amarna Period 1375-1358 B.C.	
Dynasty XIX (Thebes)	1320-1200 B.C.
Dynasty XX (Thebes)	1200-1085 B.C.

9. THIRD INTERMEDIATE PERIOD

Dynasty XXI (Tanis, Thebes)	1085-945 B.C.
Dynasty XXII (Libyan kings) and	945-730 B.C.
Dynasty XXIII (Bubastis)	817?-730 B.C.
Dynasty XXIV (Sais)	730-715 B.C.

10. LATE PERIOD

Dynasty XXV (Ethiopia)	715-656 B.C.
Assyrians in Egypt: Memphis sacked	671 B.C.
Thebes sacked	664 B.C.
Dynasty XXVI (Sais)	664-525 B.C.
Dynasty XXVII (Persian first period)	524-404 B.C.
Dynasty XXVIII (Sais)	404-398 B.C.
Dynasty XXIX (Mendes)	398-378 B.C.
Dynasty XXX (Sebennytos)	378-341 B.C.
Dynasty XXXI (Persian second period)	341-332 B.C.
Macedonian Period	332-304 B.C.
Ptolemaic Period	304-30 B.C.

11. ROMAN PERIOD   B.C.30-395 A.D.

12. BYZANTINE or COPTIC PERIOD   395-640 A.D.

13. ISLAMIC DOMINATION   640-1517 A.D.

Omayads, Abbasids, Tulunids, Ikshidites,
Fatimites, Ayyubites, Mamelukes

14. TURKISH, FRENCH, ENGLISH DOMINATION   1517-1922 A.D.

15. EGYPTIAN MONARCHY   1922-1952 A.D.

16. EGYPTIAN REPUBLIC, UNITED ARAB REPUBLIC   1952-Present

THE GODS: A WHO'S WHO

A large number of surviving texts give praise to a god, relate words uttered by a god, or beseech the favor of a god. Many gods had the form of animals. They are often depicted in human bodies, but with animal faces. These representations take place in many styles, such as in statuary, wall paintings, determinatives, and other ways. When used as determinatives, they often assist in understanding and interpreting the precise meaning of the text. Here is a brief "who's who."

SOBEK
Crocodile-headed god of the Nile. Associated with water

KHEPER
Scarab-headed god. Personification of the rising sun

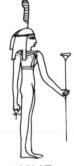

MAAT
Goddess of truth and justice. Symbol is an ostrich feather

OSIRIS
Swathed as a mummy. Ruled realm of the dead; vegetation

ISIS
Protector of Children. Wife of Osiris. Symbolized by throne

HORUS
Falcon-headed Sun-god. Personified on earth by the pharaoh

KHNUM
*Considered as god of
creation. Portrayed
as a ram*

ATUM
*Primeval god of
Heliopolis; later iden-
tified as sun-god Ra*

MUT
*Wife of Amon-Ra.
Sometimes wears
vulture's head-dress*

SEKHMET
*Lion-headed goddess
of war. Associated
with Ptah*

RA HARAKTE
*Falcon-headed sun-god
in the form of the
god Horus*

PTAH
*To lower Egypt (Mem-
phis), god of creation.
Shown as a mummy*

HATHOR
*Cow-headed goddess
of love, joy, childbirth,
heaven, music, women*

THOTH
*Ibis-headed (some-
times baboon) god of
wisdom and the moon*

ANUBIS
*God of the cemetery.
Guardian of tombs.
Always jackal-headed*

TO LEARN MORE

If this book has shown you that the ancient Egyptian language, as written in hieroglyphs can be as readily understandable as modern English, Spanish, French, or other languages, then it has achieved an important purpose. And if the book has also kindled your desire to learn more about this fascinating ancient land, its pictographic writing, and the people who lived there, then the basic objective of the book has assuredly been successfully accomplished.

In reading what Egyptians said about themselves in their writings, you can learn much more about their gods, Pharaohs, priests, leaders, commoners and slaves. Egypt had the longest unbroken cultural span in history—3,000 years.

Knowledge of the language and the ability to feel at home among hieroglyphic writings should also stimulate your interest not only in the history of these ancient peoples, but also in that of the nearby civilizations of the same period. Knowledge in this part of the world preceded that of today by 3,000 to 5,000 years in many realms of mathematics, astronomy, agriculture, political science, domestic science, medicine, literature, defense, philosophy, ceramics, and art.

One way to learn more about Egypt and the Egyptian language is to visit museums and read books available in your nearby libraries. A few universities teach the language. A book often used is "Egyptian Grammar" by Sir Alan Gardiner, published by Oxford University Press, London and New York. For books currently in print, talk to your librarian, or ask your bookseller to see the titles presently listed in "Subject Guide to Books in Print," a volume mentioning books available from various publishers.

There are numerous volumes in English, a number of which are available in paperback, carried by many bookstores and in libraries. The list changes continually, with the most popular usually kept in print.

But of course the best way to develop your interest and knowledge in the many facets of Egyptology, including its hieroglyphs, is to take a trip to the ancient sites and scenes yourself!

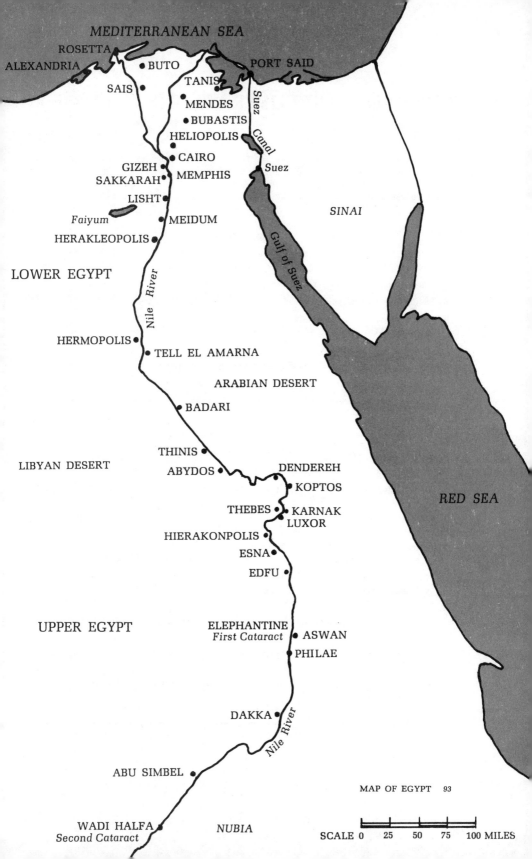

MEDITERRANEAN SEA

ALEXANDRIA
ROSETTA
● BUTO PORT SAID

SAIS ● ● TANIS

● MENDES Suez

● BUBASTIS

● HELIOPOLIS Canal

● CAIRO Suez

GIZEH ● MEMPHIS

SAKKARAH ●

LISHT ●

Faiyum ● MEIDUM SINAI

HERAKLEOPOLIS ●

Gulf of Suez

LOWER EGYPT

Nile River

HERMOPOLIS ●

● TELL EL AMARNA

ARABIAN DESERT

● BADARI

THINIS ●

LIBYAN DESERT ABYDOS ● DENDEREH

● KOPTOS

THEBES ● ● KARNAK RED SEA

LUXOR

HIERAKONPOLIS ●

ESNA ●

EDFU ●

ELEPHANTINE
First Cataract ● ASWAN

● PHILAE

UPPER EGYPT

DAKKA ●

Nile River

ABU SIMBEL ●

MAP OF EGYPT 93

WADI HALFA ●
Second Cataract NUBIA SCALE 0   25   50   75   100 MILES

SOURCES OF ILLUSTRATIONS

All photographs are from objects in The Brooklyn Museum, Brooklyn, N.Y. (identified as: B), or The Metropolitan Museum of Art, New York (identified as: M), unless otherwise indicated. Numbers are the museum's identification, usually showing the year and the number of the acquisition.

The past is prologue

Line drawings, maps and book design are by Lenore Scott